# THE LIGHTBULB THIEVES

# THE LIGHTBULB THIEVES

MEGAN PLOTKOWSKI, PhD

The Lightbulb Thieves
Copyright © 2021 Megan Plotkowski
Interior illustrations by Megan Plotkowski
All rights reserved.
ISBN: 978-1-7372473-3-3

FOR JACK AND SYLVIE
The lights of my life

1

# PROLOGUE

London is a city of magic and secrets, an ancient place where history and lore coalesce in the subconscious. We try to separate fact from fiction. However, on certain nights, the furrow between the real and unreal is sometimes blurred into the fog, and fantasy materializes in unexpected ways. The silhouette of Peter Pan can be spotted flying over the Victorian chimney stacks of Hyde Park when the moon is full. The spirits of Highgate Cemetery materialize to haunt its shadowy grounds. And, if you listen carefully, you just might hear the melancholy ballad of a lonely violin meandering out of 221B Baker Street. Everyone in this legendary town has a ghost story; an odd occurrence for which they have no reasonable explanation, an enigmatic sighting, or a brush with the paranormal.

For many years, London was at the center of a peculiar mystery; a conundrum so strange that it baffled even the brightest minds from Scotland Yard. Lightbulbs from locations throughout the city would inexplicably go missing night after night. Lights in front of hardware stores, restaurants, and even hospitals weren't safe from being brazenly stolen.

If this phenomenon wasn't outlandish enough, many Londoners reported witnessing small, shadowy figures darting through the gloomy backstreets of the British capital, contrails of mist coiling behind them.

Sightings of these illusory beings had become the stuff of legend around here. Many believed they were otherworldly, apparitions summoned by black magic or the dark arts. Some thought they were tricks of the imagination or simply fabrications to keep a rumor alive. But others who had encountered them in the flesh began to refer to them as The Lightbulb Thieves.

To discover the answer to the mysterious puzzlement that plagued London for decades and perhaps still affects the city, dear reader, you must consider an intriguing and remarkable tale. Whether it is reality or myth is not known by this author, but the manuscript detailed forthwith shall now serve as a record of this most curious story that began long ago in the deepest, darkest chambers within the heart of London.

# CHAPTER 1
## *The Girl*

"The most beautiful thing we can experience is the mysterious."
**~ Albert Einstein**

Running headfirst into a vampire on the walk to school was not how Edwin Lumière planned to start the sixth grade. The impact between their skulls was so jarring that he dropped his backpack into a pool of fouled rainwater. He helplessly watched as his prized sketches spilled out like a deck of cards, bleeding rainbows of ink into the dirty puddle. Usually, it was collisions with unsuspecting light posts or fire hydrants. However, on this particular day, Edwin's walking-while-reading problem landed him face to face with *her*. He bent down in pain and embarrassment, attempting to retrieve his soiled possessions.

"Oh no, I'm so sorry...I wasn't looking. I just...."

Edwin's stammering trailed off as he lifted his head and squarely met her gaze. His first impression of this odd-looking girl made him feel that she was from another time or place—the kind of character in the Victorian ghost stories of Wilkie Collins that his grandfather read to him on cold winter nights when the wind was howling.

The girl stood motionless before him with hair so long and white that it resembled a diaphanous lace veil cascading softly around her arms. She was clothed in a dusty black dress with ragged stockings and wore tattered black boots that appeared to be three sizes too big and only accentuated her thinness. Her skin looked as if it was woven from gauze, a cadaverous white color that was so pure, it seemed as though it had never touched daylight. She held a black filigree parasol that covered her body in a cloak of shade in contrast to other people on the street who were reveling in the unusually bright London sun. Most striking were her guileless eyes, an ethereal blue-violet that looked as though they were cut from alexandrite. Her stare held Edwin's for a moment, but he quickly glanced away, feeling as if she was studying something peculiar about him that was visible only to her.

She stood quietly and watched stoically as Edwin gathered his belongings and ran off to class. As he fled the scene, disheveled, and determined to not be tardy for his first day, Edwin could not resist looking back. He craned his neck to take one final glimpse at the mysterious person. Behind him, flecks of sunlight sparkled and danced upon the stone pavers. People dashed about in the fresh morning air. Taxis and cars buzzed past. Life on the boulevard was normal, but the girl was gone.

# CHAPTER 2
## *Snagglewick*

Edwin scurried straight on to Snagglewick Middle School without stopping and quickly entered the boys' room. By now his head was throbbing badly. He stood in front of the bathroom mirror, turned on the tap, and carefully studied his face. Sweeping his dark brunette hair aside, he identified just the hint of a bulbous, purple lump swelling in the middle of his forehead and carefully touched the mound.

*"Ouch,"* he thought as he wet a paper towel and gently dabbed at his wound. His normally healthy-looking olive skin was blanched, and his eyes were beady and wide.

*"I look as though I've seen a ghost,"* he weakly laughed to himself as he rearranged his hair to cover the injury, and fumblingly rushed off to first period.

Snagglewick Middle School was a very old place with a dark past. At the end of the nineteenth century, the building had been an asylum for England's most nervous and distressed citizens. It was then shut down by Parliament for reasons of impropriety and sat unoccupied for the next thirty-five years, overgrowing with wild walls of moss and poison ivy.

Because of its gloomy history, many students believed that the grounds of

Snagglewick were haunted by the spirits of its former residents. There were even documented reports of unearthly beings appearing in classrooms and floating through hallways from time to time which only fueled the fire that kept the hearsay alive.

Edwin had never believed in the supernatural and laughed away the notion of any ghostly visitors to his academy. However, as he considered his odd experience on the pavement that morning, he pondered exactly whom or what he had bumped into.

*"Was she something otherworldly or just an incredibly unusual person?"* he endlessly questioned himself. She did, in fact, appear quite near to the school and then seemingly vanished.

After some mental rehashing, Edwin's rational brain won. He reassured himself that it was not a vampire that he had encountered on the street, just a very strange girl.

To Edwin's delight, the first day of school sped along, and by early afternoon he was back on the avenue heading home. The walk felt wonderful; the sky was clear and bright, and the scent of magnolias perfumed the air. The sound of the occasional barking dog or omnibus engine played like background music in his head while cherry blossoms drifted softly to the ground like snow in the unseasonably warm weather. The serenity of the moment made him feel as though he was under the sway of an enchantment.

Soon enough, though, Edwin's lighthearted mood began to change when he approached the flat where he lived. As he arrived at the front of the building, he put his hand on the wrought iron handrail. He stopped on the staircase, momentarily looking up to the second story. He recognized the kaleidoscopic light radiating from the stained-glass lamp positioned squarely in his living room window. The perennial glow always seemed to calm him.

*"One last moment of peace,"* he sighed deeply. *"Here we go,"* he thought to himself as he slowly walked up the steps, holding his breath.

# CHAPTER 3
## *Home*

On the other side of his fire-engine-red front door, Edwin heard a crashing noise and then a shrill scream. As he stepped one foot inside, he reflexively ducked as a cordial glass flew by his head and smashed into the wall.

"Ugh," he groaned as his heart sank. His parents were fighting again.

Edwin resided in a working-class neighborhood in the East End of London along with his parents and grandfather. Although things could have been worse, arguments between his parents were all too common in the house. Edwin's father, Alastair, worked long hours at the city's Department of Water and Power as a supervisor but came home exhausted and had little time for his son. Edwin's once beautiful, raven-haired mother, Lenore, drank so much that she had become physically ill. Her many self-inflicted health problems kept her housebound and unemployed.

Edwin's Grandpa Bob sometimes seemed like the only person in the world who genuinely cared. Although he was elderly and suffered from various ailments and injuries sustained during the Second World War, he was always there to encourage and support his grandson. The two had a loving relationship that was even closer than Edwin had with his own parents. Many nights they would sit together in Edwin's room listening to music, playing chess, or deeply engrossed in conversation, and even though he felt that he may be a bit too old for his grandfather's bedtime stories, they were still his favorite way to fall asleep.

Grandpa Bob had a strained relationship with his own son, Alastair. Bob's beloved wife, Charlotte, had tragically been lost during the war when Alastair was just an infant. Alastair grew up with a hole in his heart, mourning the loss of a mother he never knew. Bob could never fully connect with Alastair, and the distance between them only grew as the years passed. Because of this, an ever-present ennui had always followed the Lumière family, coloring their lives grey just like the fog that so often engulfed their home.

Edwin, the lonely boy in a house full of sadness, was a misfit, a kid who had never really fit in anywhere. He was always the child who sat alone doodling or reading in the corner, dark shaggy hair hanging in front of his wide-set, dove grey eyes. Highly intelligent, he was a voracious reader and a talented artist, and at just twelve, he was the smallest boy in his secondary school class. His slight build and baby face were consistently a source of teasing and mockery from classmates. Unfazed by his peers' comments, Edwin's brilliant imagination had always allowed him to escape into the much more splendorous and interesting world in his head.

# CHAPTER 4
## *Memory*

$O$ver fifty years had passed since World War II, but Bob Lumière was still haunted. The scenes played out endlessly in his dreams, each time feeling just as raw as the last. He still heard the planes and the bombs—still saw his wife perishing in an explosion.

Unbearable flashbacks had bedeviled him every day and played out in his head a million times. If only it were as simple as a nightmare. On this particular afternoon, he awoke from one such dream in a cold sweat with a racing heartbeat.

*"No more midday naps!"* he scolded himself as he lumbered from his bed up to his rocking chair, still feeling the effects of his war injuries all that time later. He sat back in his seat and lifted an old photograph in a tarnished silver frame from his nightstand, staring into a memory.

His name was Robert, but he had been "Bob" since childhood. He was, he remembered, strong and tall in his youth, with fine features and wild golden hair. He smiled as he recalled the attention he would get at school from the girls. He had basked in the warmth of that flattery for years until one girl, one shining star, stole his heart with her wavy strawberry blonde locks and eyes that sparkled like sapphires.

Her name was Charlotte. She was several years younger than Bob and had just begun her studies in the natural sciences with hopes to one day become a physician. Concurrently, Bob was in his last year of school, finishing a degree in architecture. From the moment they brushed by each other on campus, Bob only had eyes for her.

The next time he saw Charlotte was in the library, and he didn't miss his chance to introduce himself. Over time, he would wait outside of her labs and ask to steal her time for tea or a stroll. Finally, after many blushing faces and silly excuses, Charlotte agreed.

Afternoon tea soon became their ritual. Bob would pick her up after class, and they would walk arm in arm to their favorite local café. They sat and talked for hours about everything from art and architecture to science and politics. Bob saw this as a unique and desirable quality in such a resplendent young woman and was wholly impressed; Charlotte matched, if not surpassed, him in intellect. He simply marveled at everything about her, and as the term passed, he began to fall deeply in love. He prayed that she felt the same.

It was 1933, and Great Britain was becoming uneasy about the news of the atrocities beginning to unfold in Germany and Eastern Europe. It seemed that the National Socialist Party was all anyone could discuss anymore. Just like the rest of the nation, Bob and Charlotte's conversations shifted to the threat of impending war.

Still, life carried on as usual. Bob obtained a coveted internship at one of the most renowned architectural firms in London and happily began to pursue his passion. In 1937,

Charlotte finished her degree in biology. They quickly married in the local county court and found a flat on the top floor of a charming stone apartment building with moss growing on the north side. Even though the world around seemed to be going mad, their home was like a petite little universe of their own; a shelter from the world, a warm little bear cave strung with lights. Their dreams of starting a family soon came true when Alastair was born, and they lived together, blissful and in love, until…

"Oh, Charlotte," he whispered to himself in quiet grief, still caught in a daydream.

The backfire from an engine on the street below jolted him back to reality. His eyes quickly refocused, and his senses returned as his fantasy evanesced.

If only he could hold onto his ephemeral vision just a bit longer.

Alone in the bedroom, he swayed on his creaky old chair, looking at a fading photograph of the past—the only truly happy part of his life.

# CHAPTER 5
## *Bedtime Stories*

It was Monday evening. Edwin peeked from his bedroom door and listened as his parents argued in the kitchen. His mother held and spilled a gin and tonic, waving her arms animatedly. His father paced back and forth, heavy work boots thudding with every step, leaving dusty tracks on the worn-down linoleum floor. Attempting to drown out his parents' bickering, Edwin sat in the corner of his bedroom, bouncing a rubber ball off of his wall with a steady cadence. The quarreling was enough to drive a person batty.

*"Stop fighting, stop fighting, stop fighting,"* he silently chanted.

He flipped on his small-scale radio for musical distraction, but the first thing that came on was the boring news. He moved to change the dial but stopped just before to hear a report about some odd happenings in the city. Lightbulb thieves were on the loose again.

*"What in the world is going on?"* he wondered. *"Why would anyone risk jail time to steal lightbulbs?"*

What *had* been happening was confounding the whole of London. Small figures were spotted running through the streets in the darkest, gloomiest hours of the night. Lightbulbs were being stolen from just about every building in town. A decades-old puzzle that had yet to be solved, even by the Metropolitan Police and Scotland Yard.

Edwin had pondered this mystery since he could remember, and he, too, was befuddled. The only reasonable conclusion that he could deduce was some people (probably teenagers) were trying to create rumors and stir up trouble.

*"This lightbulb stuff is a bunch of codswallop,"* he narrowed his eyes skeptically.

Edwin continued to listen to the report; it was almost as if the BBC tried to turn this strange occurrence into something creepy or paranormal. He blew out his cheeks with annoyance, switched the channel to a new American grunge band, and resumed bouncing his ball monotonously. Thirty minutes or so later, he heard an almost undetectably quiet knock on his bedroom door. He looked up just as his beloved grandfather peeped his head inside the room. Edwin turned off the radio and smiled warmly as his Grandpa Bob came in to sit with him. He eased into a chair next to Edwin's bed, gesturing for him to sit close by gently patting his comforter. Edwin jumped onto the mattress, excited to visit with his special friend.

"Would you like a story tonight, Ed?" Grandpa sweetly asked.

"Yes!" Edwin nodded his head with excitement.

"Just as I suspected," Grandpa Bob grinned knowingly.

"What would you like to hear? *The Adventures of Sherlock Holmes, Charlie and the Chocolate Factory...*?" Grandpa shuffled through his mental repertoire of their favorite bedtime stories. Edwin thought for a moment and then hazily responded,

"Tonight, could you please tell me about what happened to Grandma?"

Grandpa Bob's soft, kind face hardened, and his eyes darkened to the color of obsidian. The topic of Grandma Charlotte's passing had always been a taboo subject in the Lumière family. Still, Edwin finally wanted to know what happened, and he felt that it was time for his grandfather to tell him.

Bob paused, then removed and folded his spectacles. He looked to be deep in thought, reaching back to a time long ago.

"I knew the day would come when I'd tell you this story, Edwin," he smiled through rheumy eyes. "I just didn't think it would be this soon. Although," he remarked contemplatively, "for some strange reason, I have been reliving it in my dreams more and more frequently. Perhaps I'm becoming senile," he snickered.

Grandpa Bob seemed reluctant to discuss the topic. Still, he rooted around, and eventually located a tarnished, silver locket in the breast pocket of his flannel shirt. His large fingers fumbled for a moment as he tried to open it.

Inside was a sepia-toned photograph that Edwin had never seen before of his Grandma Charlotte, young and radiant with an enigmatic smile. The only other image he had viewed of her was the family photo that steadfastly sat in a frame on his grandfather's nightstand. Grandpa studied the picture for a few moments and solemnly began his story.

# CHAPTER 6
## *War*

The clanging, metallic chimes of an old grandfather clock signaled the stroke of midnight. The year was 1940. A tall, gaunt man placed a record onto an old Victrola, his thin hands shaking ever so slightly. He softly balanced the needle onto the disk until sound began vibrating through the large, irregular brass horn. The lulling murmur of a lonely piano slowly began uncoiling like a cobra from a woven basket. Beethoven's *Moonlight Sonata* crackled through the room. With tangled curls of blonde hair, a threadbare fleece robe, and worn-down leather slippers, the man quietly spread his musty bedroom curtains. He peered out from his modest attic window as a shiver ran down his spine.

From inside his diminutive flat on the fifth floor of an old stone building, the twinkling night sky above London faded into view; tranquil stars speckling the Milky Way with light, constellation patterns in perfect harmony; planets winking and glistening brightly. For several moments, his thoughts drifted up to the celestial panoply unfolding in front of him—spellbound. Then, just as quickly, his daydream snapped back to cold reality as he began to hear the sound of death approaching.

Quiet at first, the elegy steadily drowned out his phonograph; a low, deep rumbling, turning stronger and more ominous as the moments passed. Civil defense sirens began their mournful screams as the very air around him seemed to vaporize, leaving behind a vacuum of still and cold nothingness. In perfect synchronization with the tornado alarms, actualizing from the mist like phantoms, an arrow-like formation of heavy bombers appeared from the darkness, their menacing silhouettes slicing through the cloudless nightfall.

Clusters of bombs plummeted like a steel hailstorm and detonated randomly and horrifically throughout the sleepy city. The sound of the destruction was deafeningly loud as each impact sent shockwaves through the old stone building. The man recognized the sobs and screams of his wife and child in bed from behind his back.

*"This is a living nightmare,"* he thought to himself as he rushed back to comfort them.

He huddled face to face with his wife as they sheltered their newborn son in between their bodies. Even in the dark, he could see the transparent blue of her eyes just inches away from his own. The couple stared intensely at each other as if silently saying goodbye. Nowhere to run, no one to help; only the cold hand of random chance deciding if they would perish or survive. The piano movement played on, interrupted only from time to time by the deafening sound of annihilation.

Day broke on Sunday, September fifteenth. As the sun rose over the fog and smoke, it became apparent that most of the once exquisite architecture in their neighborhood had been reduced to twisted skeletons of metal and wood by the Luftwaffe.

The couple's home was so severely damaged by shockwaves and flack that it had become uninhabitable overnight. The man and woman stood on the crumbled pavement, holding a single bag of their most important possessions. Their baby son was wrapped in a heavy brown blanket, and they were unsure of where to go or what to do. Other people they encountered outside were similarly dazed; wandering and traumatized, eyes widened with fear and shock.

Unexpectedly, a noise startled the couple, and they scanned through the destruction to locate the source. Reverberating down one of the broken streets, the shrill sound of a police whistle pierced the unnerving silence. A British officer evacuating civilians from damaged structures frantically approached the young family. He hurriedly explained that the Royal Air Force had just reported another imminent attack and they must race to find safe cover. Just as he uttered the words, the warning sirens began again, their whining, elongated cries filling the sky. Drumfire and the roaring of propellers could be heard advancing in the distance. The officer had no choice but to make a heartbreaking decision.

"Miss, you must bring your child and follow me!" he ordered. "There is an air raid shelter close by—they have space left for women and children, but we must hurry!"

Nevertheless, the woman resisted, knowing that her husband would be gravely wounded if he stayed behind.

"Please, sir, please, I cannot leave without my husband!" she begged.

With harrowing urgency in his eyes, the officer turned to the young father, terror reddening his face. The man knew what he must do. Without speaking a word, he handed his precious baby boy to the officer. He held his wife harder than ever before, crying hot tears into her hair.

"You must go now," he whispered softly into her ear. "I love you to the stars and back, darling." The woman was vehement,

"No, no, no! I can't leave you. I won't leave you here!"

Her husband smiled sadly, then reluctantly nodded at the officer to proceed.

Just then, the ground began trembling and a pounding wind whipped at their bodies like a hurricane. The planes had arrived. The Blitzkrieg had begun.

Holding the baby in one arm and urgently dragging the woman with his other, the officer turned and headed towards the shelter, fighting the gale to remain on his feet. Just as they began to disappear from view, the sickening whistle of a live bomb filled the air.

The explosion was massive, and a wall of rock and mortar came crashing down on top of the woman, the officer, and the baby. The force of the explosion threw the young man back several meters. He lost his breath as pain erupted in his back and head. A few protracted seconds of piercing noise trailed away, and then there was only dead quiet.

Lying on his back, the man opened his bloodshot eyes and peered up to the sky. The air was so black that it eclipsed the sun, and fiery cinders whirled through its murkiness like microscopic shooting stars. As the artificial night finally began to dissipate, golden rays of sunlight emerged through the gloom, painting his body with mottled globs of light and dark.

Ever so faintly, the muffled sobs of his baby broke the silence. The man, ears ringing, eyes burning, and choking on hot smoke, crawled blindly to the sound of his son's cries. The tiny infant was lying among the crumbled wreckage, covered in dust but seemingly unharmed. Complete destruction surrounded them, with no sign of his wife or the officer who helped them.

The man, blackened by ash and soot and badly injured by shrapnel, wiped away the dirt from his baby's face to ensure he was able to breathe, quietly shushing his cries. He crouched on his hands and knees, sheltering his crying son beneath him.

Holding the small boy tightly against his body, and with every ounce of energy he had left, he sat up onto his heels to scan the war zone for signs of life. Numbed by shock and paralyzed with grief, he screamed for his wife again and again. Still, the only response was the echo of his own voice reverberating through the crumpled remains of the city.

Edwin sat silently as Grandpa Bob relayed his autobiography in the third person, almost as if he was detached from what had happened. He began to identify a slight tremor appearing in his hands, and tears welling in his eyes.

Just as the tale was ending, Edwin's father overheard their conversation. He stormed into the room, firmly demanding that Grandpa Bob speak with him privately. Edwin could hear his dad scolding his grandfather in the hallway through the other side of the door.

"You really made a dog's dinner out of that one, Dad! Cut it out! Ed is too young to hear all of that rubbish!"

Edwin shook his head and furrowed his brow. Did they really assume that just because they stepped into the hallway and closed the door that he couldn't hear them? As the sounds of their muted arguing continued to seep through the wall, Edwin plopped back down on the floor, recoiling his ball over and over, trying not to hear the details. He ricocheted the projectile harder and louder, thinking back to the horror of what his grandfather had just relayed.

*"I feel so bad for Grandpa and Dad,"* he agonized, trying not to weep, *"...and poor Grandma Charlotte."* It was the worst thing he had ever heard of in his entire life. Little wonder no one in the family spoke about it.

Grandpa Bob's memoir continued to swirl and bubble in his head like a witch's brew for the rest of the evening. Finally, after many hours of distressing thoughts, Edwin's mind quieted and he fell asleep slumped against his bedroom wall.

# CHAPTER 7
## *A Mystery Begins*

The school bell rang to begin the second day of class at Snagglewick Middle School. Edwin noted that it was another beautifully sunny morning in London. Children were laughing, chattering, and skipping around the play yard with delight. Edwin didn't have any friends in his grade and quietly walked to first period alone. When he arrived, he took his seat in the back of his classroom and began mindlessly scribbling on his new arithmetic folder.

Just as the session was starting, a disruptive noise drew everyone's attention to the door. An oversized, black bumbershoot was seemingly caught in the doorframe, and someone behind was adamantly trying to push it through. After some resistance, the umbrella gave way with a pop, and a shockingly familiar figure appeared in the doorway.

*"The vampire!"* Edwin realized with shock. *"Why is she here?"*

The same girl he collided with the previous day was now standing in the entrance to his sixth-grade class with a wide-eyed look of embarrassment on her face.

"My name is Viola Blackwell," she quietly spoke to the teacher. "I apologize for being late."

Strangely, she appeared to be wearing the identical dull clothing from the day before when he had rammed into her. She had no visible marks on her face, unlike Edwin. His bruise was now an alarming greenish-yellow color and as big as a baseball.

Some students laughed into their sleeves, while others, mouths agape, stared at her with what appeared to be a mix of confusion and unease. Noticing the disapproving look of the authority at the head of the class, they quickly drew their attention down to their hands or scrambled to locate their assignments. Viola shyly walked to the back of the room and took the only empty seat, right next to Edwin, who had been daydreaming and sketching. They exchanged glances of wary acknowledgment, and school began.

Edwin tried to focus on his long division, but all he could think of was the bewildering classmate sitting to his left.

*"I don't think vampires go to school,"* he thought to himself, *"so, she's clearly not really a vampire–she's just weird!"* he mused.

Even still, he could not stop wondering about Viola Blackwell and spent most of that day watching her in his peripheral vision. She was intriguingly strange. Other kids in his class must have been considering the same thing because he witnessed some not-so-subtle stares and heard uneasy whispers throughout the period. By lunch break, *everyone* was talking about Viola.

After eight hours of dreary studies, school was dismissed for the day. The children started to disband into another rare, sunshiny London afternoon.

Outside on the street, Edwin began his daily walk home alone, in contrast to most of the other kids who were met by parents, nannies, or friends. Just as he set off, he heard a woman make a terse comment from behind his back,

"Look at that odd girl carrying an umbrella on a day like today," she spat.

Edwin glanced back over his shoulder. He saw Viola walking alone in a curious direction, headed to a part of town consisting mainly of abandoned buildings, dirty factories, and a frightening old cemetery. No one ventured down that street for good reason. Nevertheless, he observed her shield herself from the sunlight with her lacy black parasol and disappear down the lonely alley.

## CHAPTER 8
*Curiosity*

The next day at school, Edwin eagerly watched for Viola to arrive, but she didn't show up. Thursday and Friday, she was absent again. He began to worry that something awful may have happened during her walk home through that spooky back street on Tuesday afternoon. He told himself that if she was not in class by Monday, he would voice his concerns to the teacher. Apparently, Edwin was not the only person who had noticed Viola's absence. His classmates at school, obviously affected by her uncanny darkness, began referring to her as the *ghost of Snagglewick* and *Viola the vampire*. Finally, there was proof that the legendary visitations to their academy were true, and the kids were thrilled to describe her strangeness to any and all who would listen.

Edwin frowned and began to feel bad for thinking such things about her. He knew what it was like to be an outcast and suddenly felt sorry for Viola Blackwell. Maybe something was wrong with her; perhaps she just needed a friend.

The weekend came and went, and Edwin began to forget about his unconventional classmate. He had busied himself with reading for two solid days, and by Sunday evening, he had completed *The Turn of the Screw* by Henry James. Why he would choose to read another

Victorian horror novel at that time was a mystery even to him. The book plagued him, and he awoke on Monday morning feeling tortured.

The start of the following week was dark and rainy, and the schoolyard was filled with a sea of black umbrellas and yellow rubber boots. The early bell rang, and the children took their assigned seats. To the shock of the entire class, Viola appeared in the doorway once more. Relief washed over Edwin.

*"I'm so glad she's alright,"* he sighed.

She again wore drab, black clothing—a shocking contrast with her pallid skin and hair. Her dazzling wisteria-colored eyes scanned the room. She made visual contact with Edwin, folded her parasol, and seemed to float across the floor to reach her seat. Their schoolteacher, Mr. Fenceton, turned sharply on his heel from the chalkboard. It almost seemed as if he had been waiting for her to arrive.

"Ahhh, Miss Blackwell... how very kind of you to return from your holiday and rejoin our humble class," he sarcastically sniffed.

Viola stared blankly ahead with no visible reaction to a type of scolding that would have made most students shrink down into their chairs like cubes of warm butter. The other kids giggled but quickly refocused on their homework, as not to draw the instructor's ire upon themselves. Edwin was secretly happy to see his esoteric classmate again. He gave her a slight grin, to which she returned an even tinier smile.

After class that day, the students headed out into the downpour and scattered into automobiles and under awnings, quickly abandoning the street. Edwin pulled the hood of his sweatshirt over his head and began walking home, cursing himself for not bringing an umbrella. Visibility was poor as the lusterless precipitation mixed with steam drifting up from vents in the pavement.

Out of the corner of his eye, Edwin spotted Viola, the only other person in sight, heading down that same queer pathway. His curiosity was piqued, and against his better judgement, he decided to follow.

The peculiar girl walked quickly and with purpose down the empty alleyway. Edwin squinted through the rain, scanning for his classmate's parasol in the distance. Up ahead, he watched Viola make an unexpected turn off the street and through the rusty iron gates of a dilapidated Victorian cemetery.

Edwin's heart fluttered as he considered whether to keep pursuing her or retreat and run home. Gulping down fear and doubt, he decided to continue. The graveyard was overgrown with moss and vines, lichen-covered tombstones sat askew, and the resident oak trees appeared sinuous and languid, almost as if frozen in mourning.

He could barely make out the shape of the ornate black umbrella ahead and stopped to wipe the moisture from his blurry eyes. When his vision returned, Viola had seemingly vanished into the quickly fading twilight; a trick he had witnessed once before.

He scanned through the fog. Ahead, in the direction where he had last seen Viola, Edwin noticed a dim light. He assumed that what he was seeing might be a lantern or a candle. However, as he stepped closer, he finally recognized the source of the luminescence.

Hanging from a gnarled old tree, alone in the fog like a specter, was one ghostly lightbulb.

# CHAPTER 9
## *The Entrance*

"All the beauty of life is made up of light and shadow."
~ **Leo Tolstoy**

*E*dwin stood by the imposing oak, pondering the solitary lightbulb in the gloaming of the graveyard. How it was producing light was a mystery. There was no sign of a power cord or any type of battery, which one would think necessary to produce electricity. He scanned the surrounding area.

No Viola.

*"Where on earth did she go?"* he wondered as the frigid rain finally started to lighten.

Although a heavy mist swept over the ground and obscured his shoes, something drew Edwin's eyes down to the base of the craggy tree. It was not anything louder than the flutter of a frond or the scuttling of a beetle, but he believed that he heard a slight sound–*a snap?*

Edwin reached down and blindly felt along the ground and the tree base, fully expecting to be nipped by a rat or stuck by a rogue bramble. Examining the wet, muddy topography with his fingers, he felt a large knot on the tree trunk, the shape of which reminded him of a strange little door. He pushed around on the rough bark, and it unexpectedly gave way, creaking open as if on hinges. He squatted onto his hands and knees and cautiously peered his head inside. Even though it was pitch dark, he began to make out the faint glow of electric light coming from somewhere far, far in the distance below.

Inquisitiveness got the better of him, and he carefully crawled into the small hollow of the tree, the diminutive door closing behind him with a metallic click. The entrance to the crawlway was tiny, barely big enough for a boy of his size. With his head ducked down, he wiggled on elbows and toes, slowly moving in the direction of the light. The floor of the tunnel felt hard and slimy, a mix of damp earth and solid stone. As he shimmied through the mysterious passage, he perceived it widening ever so slightly; the terrain beginning to alternate between areas that descended steeply and sections that plateaued.

He relaxed as he was finally able to inch onto his hands and knees, a welcome relief from a looming attack of claustrophobia. Edwin raised his head and peered deeper into the burrow. He began to recognize strings of miniature lights draped from the ceiling of the ever-expanding shaft. The lights, subdued and teensy as peas, softly illuminated the path forward. As his eyes adjusted to the muted light, he began to recognize details of the tunnel walls. Sparkling clusters of multicolored gems and crystals protruded from the rocks around him, and prominent veins of minerals painted the passageway with abstract patterns, giving the tunnel the appearance of a fantastical mine. As the passage widened more, Edwin was finally able to stand. Dusting off his clothes and shaking dirt out of his hair, he began guardedly walking, making sure not to stumble or fall. Larger groupings of haphazard lightbulbs dangled from the ceiling. First, only a few and then more and more until they began to resemble a surrealistic chandelier meandering endlessly down into the depths of the earth. Bioluminescent life was everywhere. Quiet sprinkles of fireflies lazily blinked in the still, dark air. Incredible arrays of glowing fungi species bloomed from fissures in the rock walls, their webs of invisible mycelia slithering underground, looking for places to spawn. Every mushroom seemed slightly different. Their caps formed odd superstructures with glow-in-the-dark colors and bizarre patterns, all overlapping like a velvety three-dimensional mural. The further that Edwin ventured into the pit, the broader and more welcoming it became. The rocky floor eventually led the way to soft dirt and then to a cobblestone lane.

Approximately fifteen minutes after Edwin first breached the tiny wooden door, he finally turned a darkened corner. He gasped as he reached the mouth of the tunnel. Further down the stone walkway, a magical-looking village was nestled into the hills and valleys of a vast underground cave lit up by millions of lightbulbs. The cavernous ceiling over the town contained lights arranged to mimic the starry night sky. At the same time, other lightbulbs appeared to be growing out of trees like electric fruit. The sight of it all was at once marvelously breathtaking and inexplicably haunting. It seemed to Edwin as though he had been transported to another realm or a scene from a dreamscape.

## CHAPTER 10
*What Lies Below*

Edwin hesitantly walked the pathway leading to the little town, terrified by what might happen, yet entranced, as if fallen under the spell of a wizard. As he approached what appeared to be the village center, some of the residents quickly deduced that he was a foreigner, and a crowd began forming around him. They looked like ordinary people, but they all had translucent ivory skin like Viola and strange, semi-opaque eyes.

The group seemed worried and agitated, and a minor ruckus developed with Edwin in the middle. He suddenly felt scared and upset; he had discovered a place that was unlike anything he had ever seen, and his head was dizzy with wonderment and fear. As the mob grew bigger and louder, Edwin noticed a swaying and spreading movement within the congregation like a dog running through a cornfield. The assembly of people disjoined, and the slender figure of Viola Blackwell appeared, pushing her way forward towards Edwin. Viola's thin voice cracked as she attempted to explain.

"Wait! Wait! Everything is OK! This is my friend from school," she glanced back at him with a look of reassurance.

Edwin realized the only other time he had heard her speak was when she apologized to Mr. Fenceton on the second day of class—now she was practically yelling.

"He must have followed me here!" she wailed.

She turned to Edwin again, this time with wide eyes to indicate that he should follow her lead and be quiet. Unfortunately, Viola's attempt to pacify the crowd set off an even more frenzied commotion. Edwin could hear angry muttering in the group.

"What are we going to do?" a young woman fretted to a friend. "If we're discovered, that's it! This is a catastrophe!"

A short, balding man wearing a bowler hat and a crooked bowtie hollered back at Viola,

"This is the worst mistake that any of us has ever made! We've lived in peace for decades with no contact from above!" he bellowed. "How could this have happened?"

The crowd erupted in agreement with the man, becoming even more hostile-looking. However, moments later, a calm yet authoritative voice spoke up from somewhere beyond the faction. They all seemed to know right away who was verbalizing, and their squabbling quickly turned silent. A very old man using a stick for a cane slowly hobbled towards the group with a cautious but bemused smile on his face.

"Now, now everyone; no need to panic, let me handle this," he raised his hand up like the pope. "I see we have an unexpected visitor…but not to worry, I shall get to the bottom of this post-haste. Come with me, young man," he urged.

The authority figure signaled that Edwin should follow him, and he dutifully complied. The crowd, seemingly pacified, disbanded, mumbling unpleasantries as they left. Edwin glanced at Viola, and she nodded that he should go. The elderly gentleman walked silently back down the irregular street, his walking stick clicking on the cold, damp pavers with each labored step. He led Edwin to a large, stone cottage with a straw and mud roof covered in soft green peat.

The foyer of the home was quaint and modestly decorated with old-fashioned-looking furniture. It smelled like warm cotton and black tea. Further into the house, they ended up in what appeared to be a small office. The room was snug and homey and charmingly cluttered with a smattering of newspaper clippings, photos, and leather-bound books. There was also a unique-looking radio that seemed to be picking up ultra-low frequencies from above ground. It produced a strange compilation of different sounds and languages from all over the world being piped into the room.

The man gestured for Edwin to sit down on a tufted ottoman. At the same time, he gradually settled into an easy chair covered in a patchwork of blankets and quilts. As he sank back into the well-worn upholstery, the man's body relaxed, and a satisfied smile appeared across his lips. His deep-set, green-flecked eyes met and held Edwin's for several seconds, and Edwin got a chance to study his face.

The old fellow had a full head of white hair with scruffy stubble on his chin. There were some fine lines around his mouth and the corners of his eyes. Still, for such an aged man, his skin was smooth and translucent like gossamer, with tiny blue veins visible just beneath the surface. He reclined his chair back slightly and gave Edwin a friendly grin.

"It has been such a long time since I've introduced myself to anyone, I've practically forgotten how," he chuckled. "My name is Gordon Wright, but everyone around here calls me the Mayor."

Edwin could see why. He seemed to be the oldest and wisest person in town.

"Now then, young man, tell me who you are and how on earth you ended up down here."

Edwin suddenly became very nervous, and a knot grew large in his chest. He cleared his throat, but his voice still came out embarrassingly shaky.

"I'm Edwin. Edwin Lumière, Sir."

The Mayor squinted his eyes and locked his gaze intensely onto Edwin's face.

"Lumière," the man repeated several times in a soft, lyrical tone. Edwin continued,

"Viola is my classmate. I followed her after school today. I don't know why I did it." Sadness and worry filled his eyes, but the Mayor made a calming hand gesture that set him at ease.

"It's perfectly fine, Mr. Edwin Lumière. You've done nothing wrong, and I actually must congratulate you," he continued, grinning impishly. "You are the first soul in over fifty years to stumble upon us. We've gone to great lengths to ensure that we would never be discovered, but it seems that our friend Viola got a bit lazy today."

The Mayor snickered waggishly.

"I suppose it was bound to happen eventually. But Edwin, please listen carefully; I implore you to never reveal what you've seen down here to anyone. Our very existence depends upon your discretion. You look like a good and honest boy. I trust that our secret will be safe with you?"

Edwin quickly nodded, "Oh yes, sir...er, Mayor. I promise I won't mention this to *anyone*. You have my word."

The Mayor appeared to be satisfied with Edwin's reassurances. He breathed deeply as his eyes flickered closed for a moment, and he seemed to sink even deeper into his cozy chair. Droves of dizzying questions swirled in Edwin's head.

"Sir, uh, Mayor, what is this place? How did you get down here? Where are these people from?"

The Mayor seemed startled by the onslaught of questions. His expression changed, and he suddenly appeared tired and withdrawn. His pleasantly round face turned ashen.

"Edwin, it's getting late above ground," he professed. "You should be getting back, or your family will wonder where you've disappeared to."

Edwin instantly knew he'd overstayed his invitation and lowered his head with embarrassment, feeling very self-conscious and foolish.

"I'm sorry, you're right, I should be leaving now," he apologized.

The Mayor unsteadily rose from his chair. Just as he stood, a puny hazel dormouse leapt from his shirt pocket, scurried up the front of his chest, and darted under his collar. Edwin tensed up with surprise,

"Whoa! What the...?" he yelped.

The mayor twittered with laughter,

"No need to fret, Edwin. This scrappy little fellow lives here with me. Edwin, meet

Figaro...Figaro, this is Edwin." The little rodent peeped his head out from his warm, snug hiding place, whiskers rapidly twitching. He curiously tilted his head to size him up.

Normally, Edwin would have been intrigued by something like this, but so many bizarre things had happened already that day that this happenstance barely fussed him.

The mayor teetered over to a buzzer on his desk and pressed a small red button. Within ninety seconds, a heavy-set boy appeared in the doorway. He looked to be about sixteen or seventeen years old and had the same pale skin and hair as Viola. He wore dusty overalls, a vintage-looking t-shirt, and had jovial, butterscotch-colored eyes.

"Ah, Mathew, there you are!" exclaimed the Mayor. "This is my friend, Edwin. Will you please escort him to the mouth of the tunnel?"

Mathew smiled hello and reached out to shake Edwin's hand.

"Will do, boss," Mathew stated with alacrity.

The strength of Mathew's handshake relaxed Edwin a bit, and the two boys headed towards the front door. Just before they exited, they were interrupted again by the gentle voice of the Mayor.

"Edwin," he called. The boys turned and looked behind them. The Mayor was now standing in the doorframe of his office with Figaro on top of his head, building a nest of hair.

"You are always welcome here. I hope that you will come back and visit us." His sly smile returned.

Edwin grinned back,

"Yes, Sir, I will. Thank you very much. Goodbye, Figaro," he joked.

# CHAPTER 11
## *The Woman*

Edwin and Mathew strolled down the uneven flagstone walking path that led out of town, kicking rocks and pebbles along the way.

"Where are you from, Edwin?" Mathew inquired in a cheerful tone.

"Right above your head," Edwin's eyes lit up. "London Town," his voice brightened. "Have you been?"

"Of course!" Mathew proclaimed happily. "I went to Snagglewick Middle School for a while, just like a lot of the kids from here. Unfortunately, I'm too big to leave now," his face grimaced slightly.

"So...you're trapped here?" Edwin hesitantly questioned.

"Well, *trapped* isn't what I'd call it," Mathew laughed a bit, "but no. I can't go above ground any longer," he said with an ephemeral smile.

As they approached the outskirts of the village, the boys observed light pouring onto the street from an open door up ahead. They discovered an assemblage of moles aimlessly shuffling in and out through the front door of a small cottage. Mathew seemed accustomed to this unusual sight, but Edwin was bewildered. He walked to the door and poked his head into the living room. Inside, an old woman was methodically swaying in a rocking chair, clearly unaware that she was being watched. Edwin hesitantly spoke to her,

"Excuse me, uh, Ma'am," he began.

The woman was jostled from her metronomic trance and appeared cross and startled. Her gray hair was long and braided, and she had piercing eyes that could be seen from across the room.

"Do you know that there is a large group of moles swarming around your house?" he asked innocently.

"Who are you to come to my house, disturb my evening, and bother my pets?" she hissed. Her response was not at all what Edwin had expected. "Now, please leave us be!"

Edwin turned back to Mathew and shot him a look of annoyed surprise. Mathew widened his eyes as if to acknowledge Edwin's discomfort.

Still, even though the woman shooed Edwin away, he felt strangely curious about her. Something about her face seemed familiar. He suddenly felt a twinge of sadness thinking about a very old woman living alone underground with only subterranean mammals to keep her company.

"I'm so sorry," he replied weakly and hastened to locate Mathew, who had continued up the path without him. He raced to catch his guide. The boys continued their journey to the beginning of the passageway.

"What's her story?" Edwin questioned as he flicked his head back in the direction of the cottage.

"Honestly, I'm not sure, mate," Mathew responded.

"She's been here since the beginning but stays to herself. I think the Mayor knows more about her—he knows *everything* about the people down here."

"What do you mean, *the beginning*?" Edwin knitted his brow. "How long ago was that? How did you end up here?"

"I'm not sure if I'm supposed to be telling you these things, Edwin. Maybe the Mayor can explain it to you some other time," he offered. "This is where I stop, bloke. The tunnel is too small for me up ahead. Just be careful, stay on the path, and you'll make it out safely."

"Thanks for your help, Mathew," he smiled.

"Call me Matt,'" his face dimpled.

"Sure thing, Matt. Hope to see you again."

The boys raised their hands to motion goodbye, and Edwin continued on the route leading to the secret passage. Crawling back through the aperture leading to the little door at the base of the old oak tree was exhausting. Still, he successfully completed the last leg of his journey.

As he emerged back onto his normal plane of existence, the chilly air of the graveyard took his breath away. He exited through the formidable medieval gates and legged it all the way home without stopping. His earlobes and nose froze, and each quickened breath created puffs of smoke in front of his face.

When he finally arrived at his family's flat, Edwin was depleted and bone-weary, but adrenaline made his heart race and his head spin. Thankfully, the house was peaceful and quiet on that night, a welcome change from the usual chaos. He swiftly entered his bedroom, hoping that no one would hear his footsteps and try to speak with him.

Edwin plopped down in bed, but thoughts and memories of his peculiar adventure continued to whirl in his imagination. Locating his drawing pad from underneath a pile of dogeared books, he impassively sketched a map of the old cemetery with the haunting tree.

Then, staring intensely at the sunset-colored lightbulb glowing in his nightstand lamp, he drew every millimeter of its graceful glass contours and needle-like filaments terminating in red-hot tips. He added every highlight, every shadow, every sparkle, and every lens flair until he could draw no more.

Exhausted and confused, Edwin eventually fell into an uneasy sleep. The day had been surreal and extraordinary, but one image among thousands kept replaying in his dreams that night: the face of the old lady.

# CHAPTER 12
## *Questions*

Tuesday morning, Edwin returned to school looking exceedingly disheveled. He had a dazed expression on his face, and there were dark circles under his eyes that made him look like a frightened raccoon. He'd been thinking about the strange underground world he had discovered and was starting to wonder if it had all been a crazy hallucination.

He reassured himself that if Viola came to class, he would pull her aside and try to get some answers to the questions pounding in his head.

*"Was any of this even real?"* he pondered. If not, he resolved to call his mother's psychiatrist immediately. Predictably, Viola did not show up to class, which made Edwin even more determined to untangle the bizarre mystery. He contemplated all day whether he should go back below ground to investigate or simply leave it be and pretend none of it had ever happened.

After school, curiosity got the better of him once again. He decided to venture back to the graveyard and travel through the secret tunnel to learn more. He secured the hood of his sweatshirt over his messy dark hair and stuffed his fists into his pockets. He shifted his eyes downward and walked briskly in the direction of the burial ground. The top of the sun descended below the horizon line, and dusk crept in; that enchanted moment between day and night when the world becomes still—the witching hour.

Night-blooming moonflower vines were just beginning to open. They gently peeled back their fragile petals, morphing into glowing white trumpets that seemed to blossom and greet Edwin on cue as he passed. It almost seemed as if the cemetery was happy to have him back.

*"Maybe this place isn't as scary as I thought,"* he considered.

Quickly locating the surreal tree with the lonely lightbulb, Edwin gingerly entered the passageway and made his way back down into the interior of the subterranean cavern. When he strode into town, the first person he saw was Viola, chatting with a few friends. Each one looked different, but they all shared similar qualities of pale skin, dusty clothes, and luminous eyes. Viola seemed startled to see him again.

"Edwin, you're back!" she said with more avidity in her voice than he had ever heard. She looked puzzled.

"Well," Edwin half apologized, "I saw that you weren't at school today and wanted to check if you were alright."

The honest answer was much more complicated than that. His thirst for knowledge was in overdrive, and he had a list of questions a mile long.

"I'm fine, Edwin. I don't leave here or go to school very often," she stated resolutely. "But hey, we're headed to a place in the cavern where only kids are allowed…want to come with us? It's our secret hideout."

Edwin was intrigued and followed Viola and her friends down a darkened trail leading away from the center of town. At the end of the walk was an enormous subterranean tree with serpentine roots that resembled the winding tentacles of a giant octopus. Mimicking the oak in the cemetery, this tree was also highlighted by a single, enchanting lightbulb hanging from a lopsided branch. One by one, the kids crouched down and climbed through the maze of roots into the interior, with Edwin following closely behind.

The inside of the tree reminded Edwin of the snugness of the Mayor's office with a soft electric glow. He observed that the entire core of the trunk had been scraped away, making it appear from below like looking up from a bottomless abyss. Portholes had been sawed into the sides, and platforms, staircases, and ropes led to nooks and crannies in the inner walls. The tree had the smell of a verdant forest, and the floor was covered with shaggy carpets and blankets. He also noticed a large pinboard littered with ancient looking maps, and a hodgepodge of wooden crates crudely stacked on top of one another.

Once everyone was settled into a corner of the fort, Viola introduced Edwin to some of her friends. She surveyed the area, pointing at each person.

"This is Ann, Roger, Paul, Virginia, Jane, Lulu, Truman, and Michael. And *this* is my younger sister, Amelia," she said with emphasis as she pointed at the last little girl.

Amelia bounced up and down when her sister called her name as if she was being awarded the Victoria Cross. Her bubbly excitement was contagious.

"I know Edwin from school," Viola imperceptibly winked at him.

Edwin was suddenly self-conscious.

"Hi, uh…thanks for inviting me here," he sheepishly answered.

Everyone seemed very friendly.

"What, exactly, is this place?" he asked.

In a flurry, all of the kids started talking at once.

"Wait!" yawped Viola, "let Ann speak first. You were saying something, Ann?"

"Yes, I was," Ann continued, chestnut brown curls of hair springing and bouncing as she spoke. "This is the kids-only hideout. No grown-ups allowed! We come down here for top-secret meetings or when we don't want our parents to find us."

Lulu spoke up next, "Right, but this is also where we keep the lightbulbs!"

"*Lightbulbs?*" Edwin was gobsmacked. "Is it *you*? Are *you* the ones stealing lightbulbs?"

Everyone instantly had cheeky smiles plastered all over their faces.

"Do you know that you're making the evening news in London *every* night? People think the city is being visited by aliens or something!"

The kids roared with laughter, looking exceptionally proud.

"Isn't that amazing?" exclaimed Virginia, who appeared to be the oldest of all the children. "We've been doing it for years and have never once been caught!" Her face radiated with delight, and she squirmed with enthusiasm. Little Amelia piped up next with spunky excitement,

"I just started taking them five months ago, and it's *SOOO* exciting!" she squealed.

Amelia was the tiniest of all the kids. She looked very much like her older sister with long, milky white hair and violet doe-eyes. However, unlike shy Viola, she was plucky and loud and spoke with purpose.

"*Vi*, tell him about the time when you accidentally crashed through that pane glass window!" Amelia doubled up with infectious giggles.

"You should have seen her, Edwin—she slid down the stairway of Whitechapel Hall holding a bag of lightbulbs but couldn't stop and landed outside on the street in a pile of glass. She wasn't even hurt, but it was *so* hilarious!"

The others began to tee-hee, but abruptly stopped as they witnessed Viola lifting one thin finger over her pursed lips, shooshing Amelia. Her alabaster cheeks flushed bright pink. It was evident that the attention made her uncomfortable. Truman piped up next,

"What's your story, Edwin?"

Edwin's life was complicated, but he spent a great deal of time telling the lightbulb thieves about himself and living in London. Although he was happy to describe the details, he ruminated on the irony of their questions.

*"It's so interesting that they are they curious ones,"* he remarked to himself. *"I just discovered a whole new world. It's like finding Atlantis! I'm the one who needs to figure out what's going on down here!"*

"I'm sorry," Edwin interrupted, "but I have to ask about this place now because I can't get it out of my head. Why are you all here?" The kids exchanged concerned glances.

"It's a long, strange tale, Edwin," said Viola. "Maybe the Mayor would do better to tell you since he's been here from the very beginning. He is a little bit like the local historian. Do you have any other questions we can answer?"

"Why are you hardly ever in school?" Edwin asked with concern. "Fenceton is starting to go crazy about all of your absences. I even heard a rumor that he has been talking to the headmaster about having you expelled!"

Viola looked indifferent and nonchalantly explained that she and the other children had one primary job: stealing lightbulbs from above ground.

"Lightbulbs keep us alive, Edwin. Without a constant supply, darkness would swallow this place. We would be instantly blinded, and sooner or later, living here would become impossible," she stated with a look of sober resoluteness.

"Kids who are small enough to squeeze through the passageway are groomed from the time they are very young to steal bulbs. That's our job until we can no longer fit through the tunnel. School is a secondary concern," she shrugged.

Edwin couldn't believe what he was hearing, yet it all made perfect sense. He told himself to take their advice and speak with the Mayor as soon as he could. The kids continued talking late into the evening, with Viola and the others recalling the many misadventures and wild tales of lightbulb thievery over the years. There was a story about a police chase that sounded like the Keystone Cops, and something about a kid named David breaking his arm falling from a ladder. Still, all the shenanigans began to blend together as he grew more and more groggy.

As he listened, Edwin began to drift off into a deep slumber. His exhaustion from lack of sleep the night before was finally catching up, and he was knackered. His eyelids became heavy, and he rested his head on a soft pillow, curling up like a tabby cat by a crackling fire. Soon, the kids' voices began receding from his consciousness, and he drifted into a deep, dreamless sleep on the floor of the hideout.

The following day, Edwin awoke, disoriented, to a vociferous argument between two male voices. He peered out from a crevice in the tree trunk. Outside he saw the Mayor in a heated discussion with an eccentric looking man with unkempt silvery hair and the large, bulging eyes of a tarsier magnified by jam-jar glasses.

The man gesticulated wildly in front of the Mayor.

"Yes, yes Gordon, I've thought of that, but the calculations still don't work," he croaked.

"I've gone over the scenarios hundreds of times, and we are still at a massive deficit in lightbulbs."

The Mayor shook his skull in utter disbelief as he tried to process the news.

"Unless we start powering down parts of the city almost immediately, we will need to find a way for the children to get hundreds more bulbs per week!" the man squawked.

The Mayor looked exasperated and held his head as if he had just been swatted in the face.

"Why didn't you tell me this sooner, Fredrick? This is a disaster! There must be another solution to this mess," he argued back to the odd man standing before him.

"Actually, Gordon," Fredrick stuttered awkwardly, "I did mention it several weeks ago during bingo night."

"*Clearly,* I did not catch that part!" the Mayor retorted sharply. "My ears are not what they used to be, my good man!"

The Mayor looked perturbed and exceptionally stunned to hear the news. He stared blankly into the face of Fredrick, the strange lab coat man, desperately searching for a fix in his head. Edwin cautiously crawled out of the hideout, surprising the two men, and interrupting their quarrel. The Mayor appeared visibly taken aback.

"Edwin? You're the last person I expected to see here right now," he sputtered.

"I'm sorry I interrupted you," Edwin looked down sheepishly at his feet. "I didn't mean to eavesdrop…I accidentally fell asleep here last night, and I woke up just now when I heard you talking."

Although he felt as if he had invaded a confidential conversation, Edwin's eyes flickered, and a teensy grin pursed his lips as a flash of inspiration exploded in his brain. He suddenly realized that he may hold the solution to their worries and again spoke up quietly.

"I think I can help solve your problem," his eyes scanned the men's faces for any reaction.

"And how the heck do you propose to do that?" Fredrick quipped, running his hand through his tangled hair, and pushing his silly-looking glasses up the brim of his nose with one boney finger.

"My dad is a supervisor at the London Department of Water and Power. He has the key to an enormous warehouse inside the building that stores most of the lightbulbs in the city. I could try to take it when he's not looking. Then, if we can organize every kid in town to meet me at the building, I should be able to open the door and they can take all the bulbs they need!" he proudly exclaimed. "The storeroom is so enormous I don't know if the department will catch on."

Edwin again stopped and watched for any indicative facial expressions from the two men. They glanced at each other briefly. Fredrick raised his bushy eyebrows and tilted his head with an inkling of concurrence. He scratched his scalp for a moment more, but finally shot an approving look to the Mayor. They both glanced back at him with big smiles.

"Edwin, this is absolutely brilliant!" cried the Mayor as Fredrick grinned and nodded with wide-eyed approval. "But will it work?" he questioned as he glanced back at Fredrick with concern.

"*Will* it work, Fredrick?" his voice quavered.

"I do think it's possible," the nerdy-looking man responded with mild hesitation, "*but* we need to begin planning promptly. The cavern is going dark as we speak—time is *not* on our side."

Fredrick awkwardly rushed down the trail, lab coat flapping wildly behind him. The Mayor turned to Edwin with kind eyes,

"Thank you, Edwin. You may just have saved all of our lives."

"I'm glad to help," he beamed.

The Mayor grinned warmly,

"Edwin, may I please ask a favor?"

"Of course!" Edwin responded, happy to be asked anything from the Mayor.

"Would you be so kind as to help me walk back to my homestead?" he queried.

"Yes—for sure!" he enunciated.

Without another word, Edwin closely walked beside the Mayor, hands ready to steady him if he wavered. The two moseyed down the rocky path into town, the Mayor's rosewood cane clacking with each step.

When they arrived back at the cottage, Edwin gently helped tip the Mayor back into his office easy chair.

With an audible, "Ahhhh…" the old man melted into his trusty recliner like a warm spoon lying on top of a big bowl of ice cream.

"Many thanks, Edwin. Would you care to stay for tea?"

"Yes, please," he smiled gratefully.

The Mayor pressed the familiar red buzzer, and Mathew quickly appeared.

"Oh, Hey! Edwin!" he exclaimed. "That didn't take long!"

Edwin shrugged as if he didn't believe it himself.

"Mathew," the Mayor chimed in, "would you please boil some water for tea?"

Mathew dutifully agreed and headed towards the kitchen.

Edwin scanned the office again—it was precisely the same as he remembered it, like a dimly lit ski chalet. The Mayor, finally relaxed and comfortable, let out a large sigh and his face softened. Edwin nervously pondered whether or not to bring up the uncomfortable subject.

"Mr. Mayor," Edwin began. "I'm sorry to ask again, but this has been on my mind since I first arrived here, and now I have even more questions! What is this place? How did you get here?"

He swallowed hard, hoping he hadn't overstepped his bounds.

The Mayor became quiet, seeming to gaze at an invisible vanishing point far beyond the wall. Suddenly, Figaro poked his head from his loose sleeve and scampered up his body into the breast pocket of his button-down shirt. The Mayor gently patted through his clothing to acknowledge the little dormouse, who was now warmly burrowed in his pouch. Mathew entered the office with two cups of steaming hot tea, and the minor disturbance rattled the Mayor's introspection. The two thankfully received their drinks.

When Mathew left, the Mayor's pensive eyes fixated back on Edwin. It seemed as if he was finally ready to divulge the secrets of the underground world. His chest swelled as he took a long, deep breath and began.

# CHAPTER 13
## *The Bomb Shelter*

"It was a long time ago, Edwin. Wartime. London was on fire. The British army was secretly building a massive bomb shelter out of a giant, natural subterrestrial cavern hundreds of meters below the city. It was not yet finished when the Luftwaffe arrived. That day was utter chaos. British military police pulled civilians from the rubble, sent the most badly injured to medics, and took the healthier people down into the shelter for safety. The safeguard was filling to capacity when a bomb detonated right on top of the entrance, instantly killing many people who hadn't made it far enough down into the safe zone," Edwin could see him choking back emotion.

"Half of the shelter caved in and was buried under tons of rock and dirt. Only the deepest part was safe—the underground cavern. I was one of the seventy-seven men, women, and children who became trapped. Although we were relieved to be alive, the other survivors and I were entombed below ground, fearing that London had been destroyed and our loved ones gone. We waited to be rescued for months. Then, slowly we realized that no help was coming, and we were most likely presumed dead," His eyes became murky, and he looked down to the floor. "After the shock and dismay of our situation faded away, we realized that we would need to build homes, find food and water, and harness sources of power. Luckily, the shelter had been heavily stockpiled with much of what we needed, so we gathered tools, rations, and other critical supplies. We were finally able to rig up this radiotelegraph to detect signals from the BBC and other news channels," he pointed at the odd-looking device.

"After about a year of toiling, we could finally hear what was occurring up in London and follow the progression of the war to its merciful conclusion," his head remained lowered as he spoke.

"Using all available materials at our disposal, we began a huge undertaking: pulling power lines that had been buried underground and creating a complex network of electrical wires that could be used to light the entire cavern, building cottages out of rock, wood, mortar, and mud, and learning how to survive off the land down here. It's remarkable, Edwin, what bounty can be found below ground. Mushrooms and root vegetables of all varieties grow plentifully. A freshwater spring flows freely at the outer end of town, providing us with water and many different species of fish and crustaceans," his eyes brightened a bit.

"As time passed, we became accustomed to living in this strange land of shadows, and slowly an insidious fear of the outside world began to grow inside of us," he suddenly looked like a little lost child.

"What would happen if we were discovered now? Would we become objects of curiosity or fodder for the news? Would we be subjected to medical studies?" He shivered as he said the words. "Staying below ground began to feel safe and comfortable, and the world above melted away from our thoughts. However, there was one item that we needed in steady supply and could not manufacture: lightbulbs. A plan was devised to dig a secret tunnel to the surface with a small, hidden entrance that could never be discovered. We excavated for years. As we approached the surface, we ran into many setbacks. There were large areas that were inaccessible due to pipes, cement foundations, and huge boulders. We even discovered ruins from the Roman Empire!" he bragged.

"We blindly dug until we found the roots of a gigantic English oak and decided that the trunk of that tree would be the perfect place to disguise the portal. The size of the secret door had to be as inconspicuous as possible. It was then that we decided that children would need to be the runners who would steal lightbulbs," his face gleamed a bit.

"When the first girl ascended, and the sunlight touched her face, her eyes began burning and her skin instantly blistered," he squirmed.

"We then realized that we had become incredibly light-sensitive by living here for so long and that any exposure to the sun could be fatal. From that moment on, children were sent up into London with umbrellas and protective clothing."

The Mayor slumped deeper into his seat and sighed deeply again.

"Did that answer your question?"

Edwin's head spun wildly with all he'd just learned.

*"None of it makes sense,"* he thought to himself. *"How is any of this even possible?"*

"Don't you miss your home?" he asked.

"This *is* my home, Edwin. I've been here for well over half of my life, and I am finally content. There's nothing up there for me any longer. The world has moved on without me."

The Mayor's story broke Edwin's heart. He couldn't imagine what horror and grief these people had been through, but out of all of it, they created something beautiful, even, dare he say, magical. That thought put a sad but wistful smile on his face.

The Mayor looked absolutely spent.

"It's very late, Edwin, and I am quite tired. Go home, get some sleep, and come back soon. We need to prepare for the lightbulb mission immediately. I assume that Fredrick is drawing up plans as we speak."

# CHAPTER 14
## *Contemplation*

Snagglewick school was a blur the following day, and when the dismissal bell rang, Edwin felt as though he might have been caught in a time warp. Eight hours had passed, seemingly in minutes.

He decided to walk London's East End to clear his head. Air raids during the Second World War had devastated its quaint neighborhoods. However, in the years since, it had gone through considerable reconstruction.

Modern life and technology had replaced the old-world buildings with skyscrapers of glass and steel that towered ominously above the river. Although it was not raining, Tower Bridge Road was wet, and Edwin's black Converse shoes became soggy and damp. They froze his feet and chilled his entire body. Resolutely, he continued trudging along the Thames in a state of deep thoughtfulness, watching the reflection of the misty London skyline ripple and glimmer in the cold river water. The evening sun hung low in the sky, casting long shadows on the pavement. Edwin contemplated all that he had experienced in the last few days and wondered if he should sound the alarm and tell the world about what he had seen.

*"Why me? How is it that I'm the first person on earth to discover this?* he sulked.

The enormity of the situation overwhelmed him, and he brooded more. A foghorn blast from a nearby ship shook him from his thoughts, and something compelled him to return underground that same evening.

Reversing course, Edwin zig-zagged back through the streets of East London to his destination. As he strode, cathedral bells rang from far in the distance, spooking a murder of crows into flight. He looked up to see their frenzied silhouettes flying in front of the palish claw of a waning crescent moon.

When he entered the burial ground through its oxidized metal palisades, he realized that this place had transitioned in his mind from a source of macabre dread into a place of serenity. A feeling of calm settled over him. Careful not to tread on the headstones, he stepped lightly through the switchgrass, avoiding uneven mounds of earth and imperiling tree roots. The towering oak tree lay ahead in the distance, and he approached it with confidence and determination.

The crawl down was more difficult this time. It seemed as though parts of the tunnel had caved in slightly, quite possibly from his own comings and goings. As soon as he could stand, he slowed down, taking more care to notice areas within the channel. Strange little bugs skittered on the wet footstones, disappearing into tufts of moss as he approached. He recognized the walls of the embankment sparkling with microscopic life and crackled geodes. He studied the intricate strings of fairy lights ambling down into the bowels of the earth and the heteromorphic outgrowths of fungi on the rocks. Lantern flies fluttered in front of him, and he stopped to hold out his hands as they curiously floated towards his palms. Somehow, he was overcome with peace. The absolute stillness and tranquility of the substratum made him feel as though he was in an ethereal space. He had been to church with his family several times before, but this place, he felt, was more divine.

At the mouth of the tunnel, he looked down upon the town. It was late; the village was quiet, and the lightbulbs high above had been dimmed to simulate starlight. Up ahead on the path, he recognized a familiar little pool of light spilling onto the street. Several steps later, he began to hear softly playing music, the hauntingly familiar sound of a lonely piano. The same song that his grandfather listened to from time to time.

He opened his ears wider and listened to the graceful, aching melody as it swept through the cool air and encircled his body. As he continued to walk closer, he recognized the humble little cottage ahead of him. The door was open, the lights were on, and the moles were meandering aimlessly like a pack of blind cats.

He peered inside.

"Hello?" his voice echoed.

There was no answer.

He cautiously stepped in and began to look around. The house was warm and comfortable, just like the Mayor's. To his left, he noticed some worn-out photographs scattered on a handmade wooden table. He slid them around a bit until one photo instantly grabbed his attention.

The light was weak, and the picture was timeworn and faded, but he had an unmistakable flash of Deja-vu when he held it.

He wasn't sure, but it looked almost identical to the photo that his grandfather kept framed on his nightstand.

*A radiant young woman with perfectly pinned curls and a sentient smile holding her newborn baby in a lace blanket. A new father standing proudly behind her, hand resting lovingly on her shoulder.*

The music on the record player turned almost hypnotic as he continued to stare intensely at the photo, forgetting for a moment where he was. Quickly enough, his reverie was interrupted as he heard a noise and twisted around with a gasp to see the old lady standing behind him clutching a broom like a sword. She looked angry and agitated.

"You again!" she fiercely scolded. "You've startled me out of my britches! Why are you here? Who are you, what do you want?"

Edwin stammered for the right words, but nothing rational came out. He held up his hands in surrender and desperately began trying to explain himself before she clobbered him.

"I'm so sorry, Ma'am, I shouldn't be here. I'm from London…I don't mean any harm. I was just curious about your pets, and I saw your light was on…I'm…so, so sorry!"

The woman looked supremely unimpressed and dismissive.

"Young man, whoever you are, you are to leave my home this minute, or I will call for the Mayor!" she screeched.

Without another word, Edwin spun on his heels. He hurriedly departed the cottage, sprinting back up the trail leading to the tunnel like an antelope galloping from a lion, heart pounding with excitement.

*"That photograph,"* he thought to himself. *"I've seen it before, haven't I?* His internal dialogue continued as he whizzed away. *"Was that a copy of Grandpa's framed picture? No...it can't be,"* he concluded.

However, as he continued loping home in the darkness, images of what he had just seen bended in his imagination like circus contortionists holding snakes.

A small, itching idea spawned in his brain and slowly began to smolder.

# CHAPTER 15
## *The Photograph*

When Edwin arrived back at the duplex in London, his parents' newest argument barely phased him. He was on a mission:

1. Steal, no, *borrow* the key from his dad's keyring so that the lightbulb scheme could move forward as quickly as possible.
2. Locate the photo from Grandpa's nightstand and try to disprove his theory that he had discovered a perfect match.

*"The odds of that being true would be astronomical!"* he calculated.

Edwin patiently waited in his room until he heard his parents retire to bed. He knew that his father usually left his keys in a chipped marble bowl by the front door, but the objects were nowhere to be found on that unlucky evening.

Edwin combed the dark house and discovered his dad had fallen asleep on the living room couch. He quickly deduced that the keys must still be hiding in his jacket pocket. He thought for a moment and then decided on a strategy.

"Dad," he softly called, shaking his father's arm, and interrupting his slumber. Alastair popped up while grunting through a snort, still half asleep,

"What's happening, Ed? What, what?"

"You fell asleep on the sofa, and I thought you'd be more comfortable in bed," Edwin feigned concern.

"Oh, yes, I guess I should get up," his father grumbled. "This awful couch is putting a kink in my neck, and I haven't even changed out of my work clothes."

His dad slowly swung his legs off the worn-out furniture and unsteadily stood up. He began heading in the direction of his bedroom.

"Let me take your jacket for you, Dad," Edwin kindly offered.

His father sleepily slid the garment into Edwin's hands.

"Thank you, Ed. Goodnight."

Alastair yawned loudly as he began his lumbering walk down the hallway to bed. Once he had disappeared, Edwin methodically felt around on the coat. He quickly recognized the mass and weight of the object he was looking for.

"Yes!" He pulled the keyring from the breast pocket. Quickly scanning the collection of dull metallic door openers, he identified the key in question along with its spare, and promptly removed it from the ring.

*"Too easy!"* he gave himself an imaginary pat on the back.

*"Now, the photo."*

He crept quietly to his grandfather's bedroom and put his ear to the door, listening for activity. Recognizing Grandpa Bob's rhythmic snoring, Edwin discreetly opened the door. He tiptoed into the room, wooden floor creaking under each step. He carefully grasped the tarnished frame and coaxed the photo out, leaving it empty with only a stained cardboard backing showing through the glass.

*"Grandpa is probably too old to even notice it's gone,"* he reassured himself to eliminate the guilt building in his mind.

He hastened back to his room and quietly closed the door behind him. Flipping on his nightstand light, he sat on his bed and studied the photo intensely.

It was the same exact one. How could that be possible and what on earth did it mean?

## CHAPTER 16
*The Key*

Thursday morning, Edwin finished a hardy breakfast of sausages and beans. He bounded out the front door, secretly carrying both the photo and the key in the side pocket of his army green jacket. He waved goodbye, but his parents didn't even seem to care. Everyone probably assumed he was on his way to school.

Electrified with nervous anticipation and excitement, he bounded all the way back to the graveyard and squirmed through the doorway that led to the tunnel. When he arrived in town, Edwin's first stop was the Mayor's office. Edwin rushed through the door, only to find the man nestled into his favorite chair, wearing a pink bathrobe and bunny slippers. He appeared to be in the middle of grooming his dormouse. Figaro was bathing in a bubble-filled ladle, and the Mayor was dusting small crumbs of cheese from his whiskers with a puffin feather.

The Mayor greeted him with a broad, upturned mouth,

"Back again? Brilliant to see you, Edwin!"

Confused by the Mayor's choice of pajamas but still focused on the task at hand, Edwin asked if they could travel back to the hideout for a meeting. The Mayor changed his clothes, and Edwin helped walk him the distance to the underground tree fort.

When they arrived, just as he suspected, many of the kids from town were already embroiled in serious discussions with Fredrick. Edwin and the Mayor approached the pack, and they all grew quiet.

"I have something you all might like to see," he grinned widely. Holding his hand out, palm up, he unfurled his fingers to reveal a solitary, ornate brass key. Fredrick gasped dramatically.

"Is that it? The key to the department?" he questioned.

"Yep!" Edwin buzzed with pride, "I got it last night."

"This is perfect! Fabulous work, Edwin!" declared the Mayor. Everyone seemed overjoyed, realizing that this far-fetched idea had suddenly become a reality. While the plans to steal the lightbulbs were being finalized,

Edwin stepped outside the fort to get some air. He was so excited to show everyone the key that he had almost forgotten about his other, equally important reason for being there that day. Edwin quietly walked away from the hideout, which was bustling with activity. He headed down the trail towards the elderly woman's house. All at once, he became very nervous, feeling butterflies fluttering in his stomach and noticing his palms turning clammy.

*"What if I'm wrong and it's not the same photo? Maybe she'll get angry and refuse to talk with me... Or, even worse, what if she tries to kill me with her broom?"* he fretted.

Searing doubt crept back into his head.

*"Do this!"* his brain commanded his legs. His sudden urge to scramble away was held at bay as he steadfastly continued walking towards his destination.

## CHAPTER 17
### *Discovery*

$E$dwin approached the simple cottage, neatly arranged his coat, and rapped on the door. As the entryway squeaked open, he peered into the azure eyes of the woman from his dream. She stared back with a look of bewilderment.

"You again? What do you want now?" she snapped.

Edwin babbled quickly, trying to explain himself before she shut the door in his face—or worse!

"Ma'am, my name is Edwin. Last night I saw a photograph in your house that looked like a picture that my grandfather has. I have the copy *right here*. May I please come in and show you?" he gulped. "I promise I won't take more than a moment of your time."

Although the old lady was dismissive, it appeared as if she sensed an innocent type of honesty radiating from Edwin. She rolled her eyes, but to his happy disbelief, she stepped aside and allowed him to enter her home.

Edwin slid the picture from an envelope in his coat, and without a word or expression, placed it into her delicate hands. She looked at it intensely for several moments and then turned and slowly walked over to the messy table of photographs in her entranceway.

She located the allegedly identical photo and placed the pictures side by side; her eyes carefully scanned back and forth between the two images.

"Look, they match!" declared Edwin.

The woman, however, didn't seem so excited. She frowned with discouragement, and he could tell she disagreed.

*"How can she not see they are the same?"* he pouted to himself.

"I'm sorry, *Edward*, was it?" she inquired.

"Edwin," he corrected despondently.

"Of course...*Edwin*," she replied.

"I cannot see that these two photographs are the same. They do look similar, but to my mind, they are not a match," she concluded pessimistically.

However, before she handed back the last vestige of his grandparents and father together, the elderly woman hesitated slightly. Edwin thought he picked up upon a glint of recognition in her eyes, but just as quickly, that spark disappeared.

"I hate to disappoint you," she said sadly, "but I really do believe you are mistaken." She paused for a long moment, "Unfortunately, I am becoming quite tired now and need to lie down."

*"All these old people ever do is rest!"* he bemoaned internally.

Frustrated but undeterred, Edwin tried one last time to explain himself,

"Miss, I'm very sorry, but this is a picture of my grandfather, my grandmother, and my father as a baby. Did you, by any chance, know them?" he begged.

"This photo appears as though it was taken ages ago, Edwin. I recognize nothing about it," she sadly replied. "I do apologize, but I must ask you to leave now."

Edwin retreated from the cottage, completely defeated.

*"I need to get to the bottom of this with or without help from that lady,"* he recommitted to himself.

Edwin headed back to the location where the Mayor was reviewing the plan to steal lightbulbs. Waiting for a quiet moment, he gently grasped the Mayor's arm and pulled him aside from the crowd.

"Mayor," he uttered in a melancholy whisper, "may I speak with you privately for a few moments?"

"Of course, my boy!" the Mayor replied cheerfully. "Just give me a minute to stand up. I think my undercarriage went numb sitting on that wooden stump," he groaned.

Edwin walked the Mayor around the back side of the underground tree and sat next to him on a rock covered with soft purple and green liverwort. Edwin bowed his head and handed his priceless photograph to the Mayor. He then began to relay every dispiriting detail of his story and the horrible predicament he was in.

"The two photos are the same! I know it better than I know the back of my hand!" he lamented. "Why would she deny that they are identical?"

The Mayor shifted his position on the stone slab while Edwin kept his shoulders hunched, looking completely crushed.

"I must tell you something, Edwin," murmured the Mayor.

"From the moment you introduced yourself, I had an uncanny feeling that I knew you; *'Edwin Lumière,'* he whispered. "A very uncommon French surname with a lovely meaning. '*Light*," he brightened his tone as he spoke the word. "A name was never so fitting," his eyes glinted wistfully.

He paused for several painstakingly drawn-out seconds and Edwin held his breath, feeling as if he was about to hear something that would change his life.

"The woman you are speaking about," he continued, "is Charlotte Lumière, and she is your grandmother."

## CHAPTER 18
### *Truth*

Although he already knew deep inside of his heart that it was true, hearing the words said aloud was utterly bewildering. Edwin felt as if he might tumble off the rock with vertigo, or faint right on top of the Mayor.

Overwhelmed with a mix of a million emotions, he sputtered,

"It's not possible! She was lost during the Battle of Britain. My Grandpa was with her, and he saw everything. He *just* told me the story! I don't understand how she can be here. What does this mean?"

The Mayor drooped his head and glanced to the side,

"Edwin, think back to the story I told you in my office. Your grandmother was one of the survivors trapped in the shelter. The officer who came across your family in the street was trying to rescue her and the baby. I guess that would be your father, eh?" he smirked.

"Charlotte and the officer were badly wounded and buried under mountains of debris when the missile exploded. It's a miracle they even survived. The officer eventually regained consciousness, dug the two of them from the rubble, and carried your grandma further down into the shelter as she fought back and sobbed uncontrollably. All she wanted was to be with her baby and husband."

"How do you know all of this?" Edwin cried out in emotional agony.

"I was the officer who saved her, Edwin. I left my post that day because I needed to do something to help. Civilians were being hurt, women and children, for heaven's sake! I couldn't stand back and allow that to happen," he sulked.

"Your grandmother was inconsolable for months. She was trapped underground with no way to find out what had happened to her family. However, as I explained before, time marched on. All of us who had been separated from loved ones began to understand that even if they were alive, we would never see them again. Slowly acceptance set in, and we began to make peace with our fate. Your grandma has lived down here for more than fifty years, and this place has become her home. However, I know her very well, and I can promise you that she has never lost hope."

The Mayor's answer stunned him.

"Why is she denying that the photos match?" Edwin asked miserably.

"Charlotte has been alone for a very long time. Memories fade. Even worse, sometimes they become locked deep within a person's subconscious. She suffered *extreme* trauma and may not be ready to process this type of news. But have patience, Edwin. Let's give her time for this to sink in—she may eventually come around."

Clearing his voice again, the Mayor continued,

"Unfortunately, there is one more thing I need to tell you, Edwin. I don't want to upset you, but I feel you should know that your grandmother's health is declining."

Edwin put his head into his hands in dismay and closed his eyes.

"Oh no. This can't be. Not right now. What can I do to help? I can bring medicine or supplies down for her. I'll do anything!" he pleaded.

The Mayor placed a kind hand on Edwin's forearm and gave him a sad but heartfelt smile, pausing for a moment,

"Just like me, your Grandma Charlotte is very old. Age is not something we can change or cure. Perhaps she will spring back. Only time will tell."

Edwin trekked home, determined to tell his grandfather the whole story; the graveyard, the tunnel, the lightbulbs; Grandma Charlotte!

Once inside the house, he didn't even bother to greet his parents. What was the point? Instead, he ran straight for his grandfather's bedroom door.

"Grandpa!" he yelled as he barged into the room.

Body spasming from the surprise entrance, Bob sharply exclaimed,

"You almost gave me a heart attack, Ed! What's all the excitement about?"

Edwin hurriedly relayed every detail of his fantastic tale, tripping over the words as he went. When he was finished, Bob removed and folded his spectacles. Edwin could see a lifetime of pain reflected back at him.

"Edwin, that is a lovely dream, and I wish so badly for it to be true," he repined. "Perhaps your father was right, and it *was* too much to tell you about the war." Edwin pushed back, explaining again, this time with more urgency, that all of this was real.

"Please, believe me, Grandpa!" he pathetically begged.

The old man smiled plaintively,

"You have a glorious imagination, dear boy. That is a gift. Either that or you have been drinking your mother's wine."

# CHAPTER 19
## *The Locket*

"Grown-ups never understand anything for themselves. And it is tiresome for children to be always and forever explaining things to them."
~ **Antoine de Saint-Exupery, *The Little Prince***

Disappointed but undeterred, Edwin headed to Snagglewick school the following morning. Once again, Viola Blackwell was not in attendance. He wondered more about her, he wondered more about all of it. Finally, the puzzle pieces were coming together, and everything was starting to make sense.

Back in class, he again heard children gossiping about the ghost of Snagglewick; where might she be, and when would she materialize again? Would Viola the vampire suck their blood or cast an evil spell upon the school? Their heartless, ignorant teasing made him angry for her as he now understood why she was so unusual.

Edwin's focus on schoolwork that day was tantamount to the attention that a tiger gives to a fly buzzing around its head on a lazy summer afternoon, and he felt extreme relief when he could finally leave.

When he returned home, he patiently waited for supper. The family was in an unusually lighthearted mood during their meal of fish pie and roasted potatoes. His parents even guffawed together about a bad joke that his father told.

*"Wonders never cease,"* he thought. *"Maybe dad won the lottery today."*

Grandpa Bob silently eyed Edwin from across the dining room table with wrinkled brows and a look of grave concern on his face. Edwin knew that he had upset him the previous night and fretted that he had inflicted unnecessary pain upon him by reopening all of his old wounds.

Nevertheless, he waited for the right moment to casually step away from the dinner table to use the loo. Instead, Edwin headed straight back to his grandfather's bedroom to snoop around where he didn't belong. He needed solid evidence to present to his grandparents—he was determined to convince them of the truth. He quickly discovered the locket that his grandpa had previously shown him and commandeered it.

Anxiously returning to the dinner table with a self-incriminating look on his face, Edwin aimlessly pushed the food around on his plate until the end of the meal. Lightning coursed through his veins the entire time and he felt shaky. Later that night, sitting in bed, he examined the decaying photograph inside of the pendant.

"Grandma Charlotte," he whispered to himself as he traced its curvature with the side of his thumb. Then, he laid back in a daydream against his wall and began mindlessly doodling on his sketchpad.

*An immense and forlorn oak tree keeping company with the dead—a broad trunk with bark grizzled by time and the elements. Serpentine roots curling around the bottom before plunging into the fathomless earth. A miniature door coyly disguising its existence like a brown looper moth resting on sandstone. A dim and desolate lightbulb; wraithlike, perplexing...welcoming.*

The next day, Edwin returned excitedly underground with his grandfather's locket. He enthusiastically bounded to his grandma's house to present her with his recent acquisition, like a mockingbird showing off its newest shiny object.

"Look at what I have here!" he proudly announced as he handed the heart-shaped, platinum-colored object to his grandmother.

Charlotte looked closely at the jewelry for a few seconds. Then, sadly, she handed it back to him with a quiet shake of the head.

"I'm sorry to say, Edwin, but I do not recognize this locket or the photo inside," she concluded with a genuinely pained look of disappointment.

Edwin's chagrin grew more prominent, but he knew that he could not convince her this way. He bowed his head, searching for an answer. Just as he was getting ready to unceremoniously leave the cottage, his grandma spoke up,

"Would you care to stay and have some sweets?" she asked as to lighten his mood. Edwin perked up a bit and nodded his head.

Even if *she* didn't remember, he was still getting to know his grandma, which was one of the most unlikely and amazing things that had ever happened to him.

*"At least she likes me now,"* he thought with a pitiful smirk. *"That's certainly better than when she was threatening to wallop me with a broom!"*

After he visited with his grandmother, Edwin began the journey home, but his heart was torn between elation and despair. He made a firm decision to talk to Grandpa Bob again. This time he would insist that he listen with utter seriousness—his wife was alive and living below ground only kilometers away!

Back in the flat, Edwin precipitously pushed through his grandfather's bedroom door and received the same alarmed reaction from the old man as the day before. Bob lurched back and grabbed at his chest,

"Blimey Edwin! This again! We've got to teach you to knock!"

"Grandpa, I need to speak with you urgently," he begged again. "What I told you before is *one hundred* percent real. I'm telling you the truth—Grandma Charlotte is alive and needs our help!"

Edwin's firm insistence was dashed, however, when his grandfather kindly stopped him again.

"Ed, these past few days have brought up so many memories and so much pain. I simply cannot keep discussing this any longer. Please let your old gramps be at peace."

Realizing that he would not convince either of his grandparents without more evidence, Edwin began thinking of ways to prove it beyond a shadow of a doubt. The following day, when his father left to take his grandpa to a routine doctor's appointment, Edwin furtively returned to the old man's bedroom. He was on a mission to hunt for anything else that he could use as proof.

Ransacking the room like a burglar, Edwin searched under the mattress, foraged through boxes, riffled through books, and scoured any other place he could think of. Finally, he discovered a small teak dresser in the back of the closet where his grandpa kept his frumpy old suits and outdated neckties. He methodically plundered every drawer.

"Nothing. Nothing. Nothing," Edwin groaned as he reached the end.

However, just when he thought all hope was lost, he uncovered a petit maroon box in the very last corner of the final drawer. Gritting his teeth with tension, he swiftly opened the wee container.

As if by a miracle, he found precisely what he had been searching for: a diamond ring with an inscription inside! He narrowed his eyes to read it…

*Charlotte, ma Lumière.*

An engagement band? His heart skipped a beat when he realized that this could be the missing link. He carefully closed the jewelry box and zipped it into his pocket.

*"If this doesn't work, nothing will."*

## CHAPTER 20
### *The Inscription*

After school the next day, Edwin excitedly delivered the jewelry underground. He knocked on his grandma's door, and for the first time since she had laid eyes on him, she greeted him with a happy, glowing face.

"It's lovely to see you, Edwin," she cooed.

*"Wow, that's different,"* he thought as she invited him to sit down. He steadied himself and took a nervous breath,

"I have one more thing I want to share, and I'm sorry to keep bothering you," his grey eyes glinted with anticipation, "but I'm hoping this will ring a bell."

He ever-so-slowly removed the dainty, velveteen box from his pocket and carefully opened it to reveal the sparkling solitaire resting inside.

His grandmother sat frozen, looking at the ring for what seemed like hours. Then, as if she knew there was an inscription surreptitiously etched somewhere into the gold, she cautiously reached down and removed the heirloom to inspect the band. Her pale, thin fingers imperceptibly quivered as she studied it intently. She put on her reading glasses and squinted as she tilted the ring slowly from side to side. Suddenly, Edwin realized that she could read the text inside.

Almost like magic, a spark of recognition flashed across her face. She turned her gaze to Edwin, the whites of her soft, bluebell eyes turning pink at the edges.

"This is my ring, Edwin," she whispered through tears.

"I know, Grandma. I know," he quietly replied, trying hard to swallow the lump that was painfully swelling in his throat.

In that instant, everything changed. His grandmother gasped aloud and threw her arms up into the air with a look of pure joy sparkling on her face. For a flash of a second, Edwin saw the young Grandma Charlotte sitting before him in all of her beauty and grace. He ran to her and gave a huge hug from his knees, head resting in her lap.

*"My parents never hugged me,"* he thought as they continued their embrace, feeling like an

infant cradled into the loving arms of its mother. When they separated, the smiles on their faces were so broad that when their eyes met, they both began giggling.

From that moment on, they were the best of friends. Edwin spent the rest of the day telling his grandma all about his grandfather, dad, and mother. He explained to her that Grandpa Bob didn't believe his story; how could it be possible that his long-lost wife had been living in a cavern beneath London this whole time?

"Edwin," she stopped abruptly, "I don't know if Gordon told you, but I have not been feeling well for some time. Perhaps it's the cold dampness here. Maybe it's something more serious, but I want you to please try to convince Grandpa that I am alive. No matter what happens, I need him to know that I'm here and always have been. I waited all this time, never knowing what happened, and then, you show up, my dear... my own grandson!" she smiled.

"And my precious baby boy is alive, and Bob...," she began weeping with joy. "Perhaps I can write them a letter," she sniffed

"I've tried so many ways, Grandma, but Grandpa thinks I've gone mad," Edwin mournfully replied. "At this point, I don't know that a letter would convince him; it could upset him even more." Edwin racked his brain for ideas.

"What if we can find a way to get you out of here?" he sputtered.

"Oh Edwin, I would give anything, *anything* for that, but it isn't possible in my condition," she squalled with puffy eyes.

"I'm going to find a way, Grandma, I promise you," he announced with firm confidence. Deep down, he didn't believe what he was saying, but he resigned himself to actualize it. He would try harder than he had ever tried anything in his life.

## CHAPTER 21
## *The Plan*

While Edwin was at his grandmother's house, he got word that the Mayor had called an urgent meeting. He hurriedly raced back to the underground tree fort.

"I love you, Grandma!" he squeaked as he ran off into the darkness.

Upon his arrival to the outside of the hideout, Edwin saw the Mayor, Fredrick, and most of the kids from town. He counted roughly twenty-eight of them.

"The lightbulb mission will take place tonight," the Mayor affirmed. "Fredrick has calculated the lunar cycles, and this evening, a new moon rises—the darkest phase. We must do this now, or the town will begin losing light within days," he warned.

Next, he relayed the plan. At precisely one o'clock in the morning, the lightbulb thieves will leave the tunnel with Edwin as their leader. The group will creep quietly through the streets of London under the cover of night, each child carrying a burlap sack with the capacity for up to two hundred bulbs.

Edwin will unlock the door to the Department of Water and Power and lead the kids up to the storage room. The whole team should make it out within seven minutes, then scatter, taking preassigned byways back to the cemetery.

"Does everyone understand?" he asked with trepidation. The kids nodded *yes* in synchronicity. Finally, each child was given a piece of paper with individual instructions and a detailed route to follow home.

Tensions were high as evening arrived. The kids began preparing their supplies like little soldiers and carefully studied their assignments. When the operation time drew closer, the Mayor gathered them together like a football coach calling for a huddle. He gave them their last orders and then handed them over to Edwin.

"Please be careful, all of you. Follow Edwin. He will guide you safely to your destination. Proceed according to the plans. We will see you back here very soon."

# CHAPTER 22
## The Mission

*E*dwin led the way through the tunnel, past the sea of embedded gems, and over and under the maze of roots and vines. When the group surfaced through the itty-bitty door, the graveyard was phantasmagoric; a shadowy microcosm of trees, tombstones, and monuments, forming a dark tapestry against the night sky.

The kids discretely tiptoed through the overgrowth while a nocturnal symphony of crickets and frogs serenaded them with chirps, trills, ribbits, and croaks. Finally, they hunched down and scrambled out through the cemetery gates, following Edwin pace by pace into the gloomy streets of London. They avoided the pools of light formed by streetlamps, staying primarily obscured in the darkness like phantoms.

The group of elusive figures silently made their way down Houndsditch to the entrance of London's Department of Water and Power. This building was the lifeblood of the city. It was huge, industrial, and menacing looking, with walls of grey stone and almost no windows. Edwin always thought it looked more like a prison than a civic building.

As they approached the imposing structure, the lightbulb thieves froze in their tracks. In front of them was a security gate with the silhouette of a guardsman inside. He appeared to see them and reached for something on his desk.

Flustered by the close encounter, Edwin heralded the kids away from the front entrance. He had been there with his father enough times to know that there was a completely unguarded postern. He brought the children around an alley, and they slipped under a chain-link fence, sprinting as fast as they could through the spotlights on the grass up to a darkened, metal door. Edwin carefully unlocked the access point, and the thieves dashed into the building. He ushered them into the storeroom where all of the city's lightbulbs were kept.

For people who relied on artificial light for their very existence, this plain room was as opulent and important as Fort Knox or the Palace of Versailles.

With a flurry of activity, the kids systematically emptied the shelves of as many bulbs as they could fit into their sacks.

Edwin observed as Viola and little Amelia worked together as if their minds were melded. Amelia scaled the tall shelves like a spider monkey, handing boxes down to Viola, who then distributed them to other team members. He caught Viola's attention and gave her a big thumbs up. She smiled back mischievously.

In a matter of minutes, the lightbulb thieves had escaped the building and scattered like rivulets of water on a pane of glass. Each kid followed his or her own predetermined direction back to the ingress at the base of the oak tree. Not merely an hour had passed when the children began reappearing underground, bags bursting with lightbulbs. As each one returned, they were greeted with cheers and celebrations from the whole town. Every resident understood the austere significance of what had just occurred.

"They did it!" someone cried. "They actually did it!"

The kids, brimming with euphoria and pride, skipped back to the tree fort, excitedly rehashing their successful mission. The chattering continued late into the night, with multiple retellings of the same story.

Unfortunately, Roger lost his shoes somewhere along the way, and his feet were frozen like ice cubes. Another boy named Tony dropped his bag on the way back, breaking ninety percent of his loot. Michael accidentally stepped in dog poop—a fact that catapulted all of the kids into uncontrollable fits of belly laughs.

Viola was quiet as usual, but she looked genuinely happy, as if a weight had been lifted from her shoulders.

The lightbulb thieves talked late into the night, still feeling the exhilarating buzz of adrenaline in their veins. Finally, Edwin decided to propose a crazy question to his new friends in the elation of the moment, the ultimate challenge.

"Hey everyone, listen!" he called. "I know this sounds insane, but can we figure out a way to get my grandma out of here?"

## CHAPTER 23
## *The Search*

"ABSOLUTELY NOT!" cried the Mayor the following day when Edwin broached the implausible idea in his office.

"There is no possible way to get Charlotte through that tunnel," he underscored with the utmost seriousness. "Plus, even if you can manage to get her out, she won't survive the sun. Don't you see, it will *never* work, boy!"

"But you said yourself that she's ill," Edwin argued back defiantly. "I need to get her to the surface—I want her to see her family again, and she can get proper medical care!"

"That is impossible, Edwin," the Mayor sadly replied. "I'm very sorry to disappoint you, but unfortunately, this is the reality of our situation."

Just then, Fredrick appeared out of the blue as if he was lying in wait for a chance to speak.

"Uhm, Gordon, there might actually be a way," he interjected with his strange, buggy eyes zipping about.

The Mayor turned to listen, looking down his nose over his spectacles,

"Excuse me?" he raised an eyebrow.

"There is an abandoned well that has been dry for almost two hundred years in the outer reaches of the cavern. We may be able to create a system of pulleys and lift Charlotte out that way," he said hesitantly, almost questioning his own statement.

"Why didn't I know about this before now?" blustered the Mayor.

"I'm not sure. I know I've brought it up at our town hall meetings several different times," Fredrick pushed back.

The Mayor shook his head and threw his hands up, looking supremely flustered,

"We need to work on our communication skills, Fred," he added gruffly.

As the Mayor tried to wrap his head around the fact that there was a potential exit that he never knew about all those years, another person seemed to materialize into the office as if right on cue.

"Grandma Charlotte?" Edwin gulped.

Everyone fell silent. The Mayor and Fredrick knew that she rarely left her home, so the sight of her surprised and shocked them all. What she said next left them speechless,

"Gordon, I've known you for over fifty years. You saved my life, and you are my dearest friend. I understand you are worried, but nothing is the same for me anymore. My husband and son are alive, and I need to see them before it's too late. I died once before when we were separated, and I will happily die again for this last chance."

The Mayor bowed his head, realizing that she was right. He, too, would risk everything for love if there was someone, anyone, above ground who cared.

"Charlotte, I can't promise you that my idea will work, but what I can tell you is I am going to use every resource in my toolbox...," Fredrick said, pointing to his noggin, "...to try and make this happen."

"I support your wishes, Charlotte." concurred the Mayor, head still lowered. "You saved my life as much as I saved yours," his spectacles fogged up slightly. "This *is* a risk worth dying for."

With the decision made, Fredrick, hair askew and thick glasses crookedly hanging from his nose, skedaddled back to his workshop. He immediately began designing blueprints for the gadget that would lift Charlotte out into the world of light above.

Days passed, and he did not leave the building. Finally, on the fifth afternoon, he stepped outside, looking spent and haggard as though he had worked non-stop the entire time.

He called the Mayor and kids into his workshop. Edwin had never been inside this structure and scanned the room inquisitively. He noticed scattered jars containing preserved animals and a microscope that seemed as though it were stolen from a high school science class. There were skeletons of all types, bubbling potions in test tubes, and endless stacks of sketches that looked as if Da Vinci himself had created them.

In the middle of the room, there was a large blackboard. Pinned to it was a detailed drawing of an outlandish invention surrounded by scribbled calculations from math and physics books. Yardstick in hand and standing proudly in front of the board, Fredrick exclaimed triumphantly,

"This is the invention that will carry Charlotte home!"

Everyone squinted their eyes to try and make sense of the drawing they saw before them. The Mayor methodically studied the proposal for the contraption. From Edwin's view, it appeared to be an apparatus consisting of a basket attached to ropes, levers, pulleys, and gears powered by a large motor.

"This looks brilliant, Fredrick," the Mayor proclaimed. "However, there is one *huge* problem...these plans call for a motor."

Silence.

"How on earth are we going to get that type of item down here?"

"I'm only the inventor, Gordon," he politely reminded the Mayor. "I have absolutely no idea how to procure such an object. However, if we can find one, I can say with very high confidence that my system *will* work."

The Mayor stared back at Fredrick's blueprint with a look of bewilderment plastered on his face.

Then, he turned his narrowed eyes back to the inventor,

"We live underground, for goodness sake! How in blazes will that ever happen?" he scratched his head in flustered confusion.

"Get creative, I suppose?" Fredrick shrugged his meek shoulders.

Even though there was a huge question about how they would obtain a motor, the building of the invention began in earnest. While the Mayor and several other adults in town met to brainstorm ideas, Edwin and Viola cooked up a strategy of their own to find an engine.

On a cloudy, dreary day in London, the two kids strolled nonchalantly to a local car dealership. Viola carried her signature umbrella and wore her drab black dress, dark lace stockings, and oversized combat boots. They made fun of their teacher, Mr. Fenceton, as they walked.

"He looks like a spider with his long, skinny legs," Viola giggled.

"My favorite thing is his weird little mustache," retorted Edwin with silly laughter. "Oh! I also love the way his left eyelid twitches when he's angry!"

The pair howled about their teacher's appearance as they meandered down Frying Pan Alley.

When they arrived at the car yard, they approached a hefty-looking salesman with a wiry red beard, striped suspenders, and a chewed-down cigar under his knuckle. He reminded Edwin of the walrus from *Alice in Wonderland*.

"We're looking for a car with *this* type of engine," Viola stated as she handed him a piece of paper specifically written by Fredrick. It contained all the specifications their motor needed to include such as torque and maximum output speed.

The large man, holding his suspenders with both thumbs, looking well-pleased with himself, showed off a large, toothy grin.

"I know just what you need, young lady! Follow me, folks."

The sizeable fellow confidently led them outside to a lot filled with all sorts of used cars. He brought them to an old, seaweed-colored Ford pickup truck.

"The engines in these babies are as powerful as you can get," he pronounced with supreme authority in his voice. He puffed out his chest with pride and his smile widened even more.

Unimpressed with the oxidized rust bucket they saw before them, the kids decided to leave and look elsewhere.

"We need to do better, Edwin," Viola complained as they slogged forward. "This is not going to work if we can't figure out something fast!"

"Ugh, I know, I know!" he responded frustratedly.

That evening, out of desperation, the pair decided to try and steal a motor. They found a big, shiny luxury car parked to the side of a bourgeois French restaurant on Piccadilly. No one was looking, and fog partially obscured the vehicle. They decided to take a huge risk and try to remove the engine. Just as they had gathered their tools and popped the hood, a tall, young valet with greased back hair caught them in the act, screaming for the police in broken English. Edwin and Viola scurried away into the misty darkness like chipmunks absconding from a hawk's talons.

Later that same night, while wandering around aimlessly on the East End, they ambled right into a speedboat resting on wooden blocks in someone's front yard, an easy target!

"This engine should definitely do the trick," Edwin decided.

The kids had almost unbolted the motor when they heard the shouting of profanities and saw a pudgy man quickly approaching. He was wearing only underpants and an open robe that slid from his body more and more, the harder he raced.

"Stop them!" he shrieked, shaking his fist wildly.

Again, the kids sprinted away like prey, vanishing very quickly into some unruly hedgerows on the outskirts of Mile End Park.

*"Sometimes it does help to be small,"* mused Edwin.

The pair traipsed back to the cemetery, thoroughly chagrined.

"This will never work!" Edwin harumphed.

His tummy twisted as he realized he might not be able to fulfill his promise to Grandma Charlotte, which was an excruciating thought. The worry about that possibility stayed with him all night, and he had an eerie premonition that his grandma would pass on before she could see her husband and son. He tossed and turned for hours but could not shake that awful feeling for the rest of the night.

In the morning, Edwin woke up looking as if he hadn't slept at all. His eyes were sore and watery. He had a dour complexion, and his dark hair was flipped up as if he had stuck his finger into an electrical outlet. He hastily pulled himself together and went to search for Viola.

He needed her to come with him to the Mayor's cottage to pitifully share their nonsuccess. When he located her, the two of them rounded up several of the other lightbulb thieves, and the group plodded to the door of the home. The Mayor greeted the dismayed collection of children.

"We tried so hard," Viola whimpered to him, "but we just couldn't do it," she drooped her head in resignation.

The situation was beginning to seem hopeless when a squeaky voice spoke up from the foyer,

"I know where we can find an engine right down here!"

The group looked around to identify the person speaking. To everyone's amazement, they realized that it was coming from little Amelia Blackwell.

Viola scrunched her brow and looked at her baby sister with stunned surprise.

"Amelia...," the Mayor was confused. "What are you saying? What engine?"

"There is a World War II-era fighter plane half-buried in the side of a cliff in the outer regions of the cavern," Amelia replied confidently. "I go and look at that airplane sometimes. It reminds me of why we are down here, and I think about the man who piloted it during the war. I wonder about his family and friends. Do they even know what happened to him? What was his name? Whomever he was, he's a hero to me."

Not many people besides Viola and the Mayor knew that the little girl was named after Amelia Earhart, and she dreamed of becoming a pilot. She studied books on aircrafts and even taped drawings of her favorite models over her bed. Amelia had been quiet the whole time and what came out of her mouth was shocking. The Mayor listened to her thoughtful words,

"This is incredible, Amelia! I cannot wait to see your discovery," he chirped.

"If you will, please take us there now. We haven't a moment to spare!"

## CHAPTER 24
### *The Airplane*

*A* remarkable and unlikely procession of characters began hiking to the outer lands of the cave: the Mayor hobbling by cane, Fredrick with his typical disheveled lab coat, static electric hair, and google-eyes, and the lightbulb thieves with Amelia at the helm. They carried an assortment of picks, shovels, lanterns, and tools.

As they approached what seemed like the end of the world, they began to see the uncharted and mysterious territory that existed beyond. It was a perplexing maze of vast underground tunnels and caves that seemed to go on forever. Some of the trails were perilous, with steep bluffs that dropped off into dark nothingness. There were subterranean waterways housing strange phosphorescent organisms and hot springs that gave off vapors of sulfurous steam. Stalactites and stalagmites resembling sharp teeth made them feel as though they were inside the mouth of a carnivorous dinosaur.

The group carefully navigated a steep precipice. A forest of dagger-like crystals gave off an eerie but radiant glow from hundreds of meters below.

'Wow, that is absolutely stunning," Edwin marveled.

"Yes, indeed," said Fredrick, "but its divine beauty masks the horrible reality that a fall from this ledge would result in an unimaginably gruesome and painful casualty."

"Thanks, Fredrick," Edwin shivered, "that makes me feel *so* much better."

At the apex of the curve, Amelia pointed to the terrain up above. Everyone stopped in reverent silence. Just as she had said, jutting out from the cliff wall was the nose cone, propeller, and part of a wing from a British fighter plane. Amelia pointed out certain features of the paint, metal, and rivets, concluding,

"From what I can see, this is a Hawker Hurricane with a Rolls Royce V12 engine. It should have about 1,300 horsepower. Will that be enough?" she innocently questioned with a lively little trill. Everyone's jaw dropped in unison.

"How does she know this stuff?" Fredrick looked to the Mayor.

The Mayor always knew that Amelia loved airplanes, but this was a different level altogether and he shrugged in disbelief.

Fredrick, dumbstruck, nodded his head back at Amelia as if to say,

"Yes, this is *definitely* enough."

Viola proudly took her sister's hand and Amelia beamed back with pride.

Becoming makeshift archeologists, the rag-tag team began the solemn and challenging task of unearthing the fallen British fighter. The metal was lodged so firmly into the bedrock that the Mayor had a dreadful sense that this plan might all be for naught. He kept his worry to himself as he anxiously looked on.

At a certain point in the dig, the troop realized that they must apply pressure to dislodge the nose of the aircraft from the mountain. Someone needed to climb up to the propeller and use their body weight to pull it from the earth. Mathew raised his hand and willingly volunteered. Everyone knew the risk he was taking; if he slipped, he would plummet into a sea of crystalline daggers.

Undeterred, Mathew slowly climbed the rock wall up to the propeller. Tensions were high as he reached the sharp metal blades and held on with both hands, his body dangling in space. Seconds passed, and nothing happened.

Suddenly, with no warning, the propeller creaked and turned, causing Mathew to lose his grip with one hand. The group collectively gasped in horror as his body spun and swayed above the treacherous forest of knives below. Yet, he stayed calm and grabbed hold of the metallic edge again.

As he continued to hang, the front of the airplane appeared to gradually come loose.

Then, millimeter by millimeter, it began liberating from the earth. Mathew carefully worked his way back down to the ground, receiving applause from the kids and huge compliments from the Mayor.

"You did it, my boy! Well done!" the Mayor cheered.

"Hooray for Matt!" bellowed Paul.

The entire group whooped and wailed as Mathew tried to hide his blushing cheeks.

The disengaged nose cone was meticulously removed, exposing the inner workings of the machine. Amelia pointed to where the engine was nestled, and the team, all working together, carefully lowered it to the ground.

# CHAPTER 25
## *Practice*

With the motor secured, the invention neared completion. Fredrick began a series of experimental test runs to calibrate the apparatus. Edwin and Viola constructed a dummy the same shape and weight as Grandma Charlotte, complete with a flowered dress and hat, courtesy of Viola. The mannequin was hoisted into a large wicker basket, formerly a storage bin for forgotten potatoes, and the engine was fired up.

The first attempt was a complete disaster. The contraption lifted the dummy three-quarters out of the shaft when the rope broke, and the mannequin plummeted from a great height. It landed in a crumpled pile at the bottom of the well. Everyone watching winced with discomfort, picturing the real-life Charlotte having a perilous fall into the rocks below.

The second endeavor was not any better. The rope was pulled startlingly fast, and the figure was launched out of the pit like a cannonball. A collective gasp could be heard from the people below who envisioned a living person in place of the dummy. Trials continued around the clock, with Fredrick learning from each mistake and making puny tweaks until the machine worked flawlessly and the weight inside could be lifted safely from the chasm.

While the experiments were being completed and the apparatus was fine-tuned, Edwin realized that he had been away from home for days and had missed *a lot* of school. He dreaded the consequences, but he simply couldn't worry about that now. Instead, he needed to keep his focus on helping his grandmother. His parents rarely paid attention to him anyway; they probably thought he was staying with a friend.

## CHAPTER 26
*Panic*

Above ground in London, however, the realization that Edwin was gone did not escape his parents and grandfather. They hadn't seen him for almost a week, and Snagglewick had been persistently calling to inquire about his absences. As time passed without his presence at their small flat in London, Edwin's family became more and more frantic. Their dear, sweet boy had been missing, and no one realized it for days.

Edwin's mother, Lenore, called the Metropolitan Police Department in sheer panic. A chief constable came to the house to escort her to the station. She was to file a missing person's report, give a detailed description, and answer a series of questions that might be helpful to find him. While Lenore traveled to the central office, an investigation was initiated. Two deputy inspectors were sent out into the streets to begin the search for Edwin.

Meanwhile, Bob started to desperately feel that he must do something on his own to help find Edwin. In his mind, he began putting the pieces together, remembering what Edwin had told him so many times but, he had refused to listen.

*"The graveyard, the tunnel, Charlotte...."*

Bob bustled as fast as his shaky legs could carry him into the chartreuse-tinged kitchen. His son sat quietly at the table, looking as though he had been trampled by a gang of wild buffalo.

The old man pushed his way through the splintery door and began frenetically explaining to Alastair what may have happened to Edwin. The boy had been telling him all along, yet his stubborn mind would not even believe his own grandson.

Finally, Alastair realized that his father might be on to something, and he sprang into action. He combed through Edwin's bedroom, looking for evidence, searching for anything that might help locate him.

Edwin's room was cluttered with books, drawings, and unfolded clothes. Alastair knelt down, scanning each one of them for a clue about where his son could be. Within a few minutes, he found a small, hand-drawn map of a graveyard and several abstract sketches of lightbulbs—just another smattering of Edwin's doodles, or something more meaningful? He felt in his gut that the map might lead them to his son.

As Alastair rummaged through Edwin's bedroom, Bob conducted a search of his own. First, he scanned his own bedroom. Everything seemed normal until he finally noticed that the priceless, framed photo from his nightstand was missing. A pang of anxiety gripped his stomach and he felt woozy.

How did he not see that before? He dug deeper. His locket was missing! And the ring?

"Please no, not the ring!"

He desperately checked the bottom drawer of the dresser in his closet and found that the jewelry, too, had disappeared—his only mementos of Charlotte...gone.

*"Why in blazes did Edwin take them?"* he puzzled.

As he continued to ponder the evidence before him, he began to realize that Edwin wasn't spinning a tall tale after all. Alarm swelled in his chest, and at that moment, he had an epiphany so obvious that he could picture it in his mind as if it was laid out before him in black ink.

"Crikey! He wasn't making this up!" he gasped aloud.

The men agreed that they could not sit idle any longer while their beloved boy was missing. They both put on heavy tweed coats and deerstalker caps and headed out into the foggy streets of London carrying flashlights and holding Edwin's hand-drawn diagram as a guide. When they exited the flat, they ran right into the two policemen who had been assigned to the case, Lieutenant Crankshaw and constable Shufflebottom. Crankshaw had the most enormous handlebar mustache they had ever seen, and Shufflebottom smelled like tobacco and stale coffee.

"Officers, please, we need your assistance!" Bob pleaded. "Will you follow us? We may have discovered where my grandson ran off to."

The four men followed Edwin's map into the cemetery with trepidation. Ambling around a graveyard in the middle of the night was not anyone's idea of fun. In fact, the experience was nerve-racking for all of them. Everyone was on edge as all four flashlight beams darted between sunken obelisks, weather-beaten headstones, and gloomy sepulchers.

As they scrutinized the land, they began to recognize features from Edwin's map. A foolishly ornate Baroque cross, a gothic angel weeping in the mist, and a formerly grand mausoleum covered in graffiti. Relief finally came when they recognized the oak tree with the phantasmal lightbulb in the distance.

"Up ahead! There it is—the lightbulb tree!" Constable Shufflebottom proclaimed with triumph.

The men rushed towards the old timber and began pushing and kicking on its unwieldy trunk. Then, finally, the miniscule door slowly scraped open. Alastair and Bob put their stomachs down on the cold, wet grass, shined their flashlights into the black hole, and cried out for Edwin.

The two bobbies, standing close by, traded bemused smiles.

"Mr. Lumière, Sir…are you suggesting that your son is *inside* of this tree?" Crankshaw sarcastically posited, trying unsuccessfully to hold back his laughter.

"That is *exactly* what I am suggesting, lieutenant!" Alastair snapped back defiantly.

The policemen snickered at the absurdity of the idea, but they continued to humor the two men.

Finally, out of utter desperation, Bob tried to squeeze his cranium into the opening. The sight of the old man lying down on his belly with his head lodged inside of an old tree made the two officers chortle loudly. They attempted to disguise their Cheshire Cat grins but found it almost impossible.

"Edwin! his voice echoed into the great oak. Are you in there? "It's your Grandpa Bob," he wailed. "Please come out!"

There was no response. The only sound that could be heard in return was giggles and guffaws from the police officers who were having a hard time holding themselves together.

Eventually, with supreme frustration, Bob and Alastair realized that their plan was not working.

They pleaded with the policemen to wait by the tree in case Edwin showed up; they would rush back home and see if he resurfaced.

## CHAPTER 27
## *Reunion*

"Even in the bruised deep dark, hope creates a tiny spark to lead you out."
~ **Angie Weiland-Crosby**

The whole town gathered at the base of the fountainhead for the momentous occasion. There was electricity in the air, and everyone felt it. Even though it was nighttime, Charlotte wore all black with a big floppy hat and dark sunglasses.

"One can never be too careful," she reminded the children.

She grasped only a small rucksack containing her most treasured belongings in one arm and her favorite pet mole, Falcon, in the other. Falcon was black and rust, a most unusual color pattern for a *Talpa*. The kids giggled and cooed as the curious creature made quirky barking sounds to show his enthusiasm.

The Mayor chivalrously took Charlotte's hand and helped her into the basket. He was ceremoniously dressed in the same coat and cap that he wore when he saved her life. His uniform was snug—*no*, uncomfortably tight, but he felt that wearing it was only appropriate under the circumstances—he was a man of decorum, after all. They exchanged a long-lasting, heartfelt embrace, and the Mayor realized that this was their swan song; the last time they would see each other in this lifetime.

He stepped back, gathered himself, and

like a general calling for a charge, instructed Fredrick to start the engine. Fredrick, giving a respectful bow, ignited the old machine. The motor coughed and hiccupped, spewing smoke and the smell of pungent benzene fuel into the air as the propeller slowly began its revolutions. Finally, the ropes became taut, and the capsule levitated from the bottom of the well, swaying and spinning ever so slightly.

The Mayor took off his military-peaked visor hat. Figaro was relaxing on his head nibbling on a peanut and didn't seem to notice that his hiding place had been exposed. No one even raised an eyebrow. Edwin assumed that this was a common sight around the village, similar to keeping moles as pets.

Using his cap, the Mayor began waving goodbye, inspiring the townspeople to do the same.

"Goodbye, Charlotte!" a voice rang from the crowd, which inspired others to call out to her as well.

Charlotte signaled back and blew kisses as she began her ascent with an ear-to-ear grin. The Mayor marveled at how completely at ease she was in such a precarious situation.

Edwin, Viola, and several of the lightbulb thieves waited anxiously at the edge of the ancient well, gripping onto it with white knuckles as they peered down. Nearby, a family of Great Horned Owls stood watch from a weeping willow, their glowing yellow eyes unblinking in the nightscape. They, too, seemed to want to bear witness to the extraordinary affair that was unfolding.

It took fifteen agonizing minutes of slow rising as the onlookers collectively held their breath. Then, at last, the basket reached the mouth of the abyss. It cleared the stone wall, and the kids carefully helped Edwin's grandmother out of the receptacle and into a waiting wheelbarrow filled with cushions. Once she was secured, the children began speeding down Petticoat Lane towards Edwin's house. Two kids jogged on each side of the wheelbarrow in case it tipped over, a bizarre sight, to say the least. Charlotte's bonnet whipped in the wind as she laughed with glee. Falcon crawled onto her shoulder and audibly squealed. Edwin could not even imagine the range of emotions that she was experiencing at that moment. Seeing modern London, feeling the wind on her face, breathing in the fresh night air...reuniting with her long-lost family for the first time in half a century!

*"This is the most stupidly ridiculous and brilliantly insane thing I've ever done,"* he smiled.

When they finally arrived at the flat, Edwin noted that the stained-glass lamp in his living room window had been extinguished. Its ever-present, polychromatic light had always watched over his home like one of the gargoyles of Notre Dame. Somehow the darkened beacon gave him a feeling of dread—no one was home. Something was definitely wrong.

The lightbulb thieves helped Charlotte out of the wheelbarrow and walked her into the duplex. Entering through the red door and stepping into his own home felt eerie for Edwin. It was drafty and cold, appearing almost as though it had been abandoned. He didn't yet realize it, but his entire family and the authorities were out looking for him. Grandma Charlotte was gently helped onto a bed in the rear of the home by Edwin and his friends. They all insisted that she lie down and rest after what she had just endured. The old woman curled onto her side, relaxed into the down comforter, and looked up at the children gathered around the bed.

"Thank you for helping me. I love you, and I will miss you all *so* very much."

"We'll come back to visit—don't you worry, Charlotte!" reassured Ann.

The lightbulb thieves quickly said their goodbyes and excused themselves, receding out into the midnight mist.

Edwin walked to the living room window and pulled the metal cord to reilluminate the lamp. He leaned forward and peered at the street below. The road was still and vacant except for a pair of sylph-like stray cats skulking around some rubbish bins on the curb. The guttural croak of a raven perched in a sycamore tree sent an ominous chill down his spine and he abruptly turned away, feeling as if the bird was a bad omen.

*"Where are they?"* he fretted.

He looked across the room and was surprised to see Viola standing by the dining room table. He assumed she had left. When he saw her sweet, pale face, he forgot about his worries for a moment, and gratitude poured from his chest. He walked over to give her a hug.

"I owe you *everything*, Vi," he whispered to the girl who, only weeks before, he had suspected of being some type of supernatural being. However, as he reflected on that idea just a bit more, it occurred to him that she was indeed supernatural. It was because of her that he had discovered Grandma Charlotte and rewrote his family's history. She had inadvertently led him to glimpse mystery and wonder that he never thought could have existed, and she had reignited love into his heart. What could possibly be more magical?

As she stepped back from their hug, Viola glanced back at Edwin with a nostalgic smile.

"See you around, Edwin," she grinned with a lively little sparkle in her eyes. Then, without another word, she silently slipped through the door and vanished into the night.

*"The ghost of Snagglewick,"* he shook his head with incredulity, *"more like the angel."*

Once Viola left, gripping feelings of nervousness and guilt crept back into Edwin's mind. He brooded silently,

*"I was gone for days! They probably think I'm lost or dead."*

He plopped down on one side of his faux-leather couch and listened to the monotonous ticks of his family's antique grandfather clock for what seemed like an eternity.

*"Stay calm; they'll come back. Everything will be OK,"* Edwin gave himself an unsuccessful pep-talk as he grappled with dark and disturbing thoughts.

At some point later, he couldn't tell if it was minutes or hours, Edwin began to hear voices approaching from the stairs. He lifted his head and focused intently on the noise. Yes, the sounds were advancing towards his front door, and he stood up from the couch just as it swung open.

His dad and grandfather had returned from their failed rescue mission looking like detectives from 1890. However, unlike the very polished and civilized characters from Arthur Conan Doyle, they looked bedraggled and boorish, their faces so covered in dirt that they resembled coal miners. Their clothing was filthy and wet, and the expressions on their faces told Edwin exactly how they were feeling—weary and hopeless.

Edwin's stress instantly melted away. He had *never* been so excited to see them. The two men unceremoniously entered the flat, mumbling incoherently to one another. They were utterly unaware that Edwin was only steps away from them. Suddenly, Alastair glanced up and saw his son standing before him. He gasped with astoundment and shock, and his eyes came back to life, sparkling like firecrackers.

"Edwin! You're here; you're safe!" The two men scrambled to grab hold of him as if he might again disappear. "Where were you? We were so worried!" his father queried.

Edwin tried to respond but quickly realized that only one person had the answers they needed. From a corner of the living room, they all heard a loud squeak and looked down just in time to see a mini, rodent-like animal scuttle across the floor. The two men jumped back in shock and dismay.

"Ehh!" screamed Alastair. "Rats again?"

"That's a mole, Dad. His name is Falcon," Edwin interjected.

Alastair didn't react; he was still considering which type of animal was less offensive running loose in his home; a rodent or an insectivore.

"He won't bite."

A disembodied female voice spoke up from somewhere in the darkness beyond them.

Out of the shadows in the hallway, the narrow figure of a woman appeared. She slowly stepped forward until lamplight illuminated her face. Still achingly beautiful with long grey hair and the haunting eyes of a ghost, a person from a dream, an apparition materialized.

Bob's knees buckled, and Edwin's father caught him under the arms before he fell. The room began to spin as a storm of joy and sorrow and disbelief rained down over them. No words were spoken. Charlotte, Bob, and Alastair embraced as space and time evanesced.

# CHAPTER 28
## *Peace*

> "All precious things discovered late
> To those that seek them issue forth,
> For Love in sequel works with Fate,
> And draws the veil from hidden worth"
> **~ Alfred Lord Tennyson**

The Lumière home came back to life on that day. The sorrow that used to hang heavy like a dark raincloud vaporized into the ether, never to be seen again. Alastair and Lenore finally made peace; their constant arguing stopped, and in its place, there was laughter. Music wafted and whorled through the air, and before long, it felt as though Charlotte had always been with them; in some ways, they realized, she always had.

Viola never returned to Snagglewick, and her legend faded into middle school folklore.

Edwin missed all of his friends but was hesitant to go back underground. It wasn't that he had lost any affection for them. In fact, quite the opposite; he thought of them constantly, but the strings to his heart pulled him to stay with his family. The lightbulb thieves had not been seen for months, and the salacious news reports disappeared from the headlines as the media found new and more exciting sources of gossip and scuttlebutt.

Edwin and his parents carefully transformed his grandparents' bedroom into a safe, dark space where Grandma Charlotte could live peacefully without fear of being burned by sunlight. Black velvet curtains were installed to cover the windows, and myriad lightbulbs were gracefully draped from the ceiling, giving the room the feeling of celestial tranquility.

Finally, after fifty-odd years, Grandpa Bob and Grandma Charlotte laid side by side in bed, holding hands and gazing up together at the delicate, glass sky of stars. Bob closed his eyes and started to hear the sound of planes again, a phantom that had followed him since he was a young man. He turned to look at his courageous wife lying beside him—the survivor, the astronaut, the time traveler. Charlotte tilted her head and revealed the most beautiful smile he had ever seen.

"Time. Stop. Now." he commanded the universe.

As his focus returned to the sea of lightbulbs above, the hum of propellers melted away and was completely replaced by the song of their youth. Spheres of light began to blur and morph, and as he stared at the ceiling, the transcendent midnight sky appeared in its place. Clearer and more spectacular than he had ever seen, the moon, the planets, and the stars gazed down lovingly—no more nightmares.

While the last tender notes of the *Moonlight Sonata* trailed off, the cosmos of their room slowly faded to black as husband and wife fell asleep together, once again.

# EPILOGUE

While most of the population may relegate this tale to the world of fantasy and ghost story lore, there are a small number of people who believe it to be accurate. Fairy tales and urban legends are rarely accepted by those who have not experienced the unexplainable, so it is quite likely that you, too, will disregard this narrative and assign it to the realm of allegory.

However, one day, you might catch a glimpse of an elusive, shadowy figure whisking through the gloomy streets of London on a dark, rainy night and remember this account. You may dismiss it as fantasy or your eyes playing tricks on you.

But maybe, just maybe, you will smile and marvel at the beauty and bewitchery of the mysterious—the unknowable.

After all, dear reader, London *is* a city of magic and secrets.

Megan Plotkowski earned her PhD in Molecular Biology and Biochemistry from UCLA in 2008. She has been a research scientist, a technology consultant, an inventor, a stay-at-home mom, a wannabe wine snob, a pretty good cook, an artist, and a writer. She crashed through a plate glass window in a runaway cardboard box when she was ten, survived a bottle to the head during a bar fight in college, and is a self-proclaimed margarita connoisseur. *The Lightbulb Thieves* was inspired by her secret obsession with all things dark, strange, and mysterious that no one knew about until now. Megan lives in Los Angeles with her two kids and their giant Doberman. Connect with her on Instagram @thelightbulbthieves